Elsie at the World's Fair

The Original Elsie Classics

Elsie Dinsmore
Elsie's Holidays at Roselands
Elsie's Girlhood
Elsie's Womanhood
Elsie's Motherhood
Elsie's Children
Elsie's Widowhood
Grandmother Elsie
Elsie's New Relations
Elsie at Nantucket
The Two Elsies
Elsie's Kith and Kin
Elsie's Friends at Woodburn
Christmas with Grandma Elsie
Elsie and the Raymonds
Elsie Yachting with the Raymonds
Elsie's Vacation
Elsie at Viamede
Elsie at Ion
Elsie at the World's Fair
Elsie's Journey on Inland Waters
Elsie at Home
Elsie on the Hudson
Elsie in the South
Elsie's Young Folks
Elsie's Winter Trip
Elsie and Her Loved Ones
Elsie and Her Namesakes

Elsie at the World's Fair

Book Twenty of
The Original Elsie Classics

Martha Finley

CUMBERLAND HOUSE
NASHVILLE, TENNESSEE

Elsie at the World's Fair
by Martha Finley

Published by Cumberland House Publishing, Inc.,
431 Harding Industrial Drive, Nashville, Tennessee 37211.

Cover design by Bruce Gore, Gore Studios, Inc.
Photography by Dean Dixon Photography
Hair and Makeup by Calene Rader
Text design by Heather Armstrong

Printed in the United States of America
1 2 3 4 5 6 7 8 – 04 03 02 01 00

Chapter First

Hugh Lilburn was very urgent with his betrothed for a speedy marriage, pleading that as her brother had robbed him and his father of their expected housekeeper—his cousin Marian—he could not long do without the wife who was to supply her place. Her sisters, Isadore and Virginia, who had come up from the far South to be present at the ceremony, joined with him in his plea for haste. They wanted to see her in her own home, they said, and that without remaining too long away from theirs. Ella finally yielded to their wishes so far as to complete her preparations within a month after their homecoming from the North.

The wedding was a really brilliant affair and was followed up by parties given by the different members of the family connection. No bridal trip was taken, neither bride nor groom caring for it, and Hugh's business requiring his presence at home.

A few weeks later Calhoun Conly went North for his bride. Some festivities followed his return. Then all settled down for the winter, Harold and Herbert Travilla taking up their medical studies with Dr. Conly, and Captain Raymond's pupils resuming such of their lessons as had been dropped for the time, though the wedding festivities had not been allowed to interfere with them, as—with the exception of Marian, now Mrs. Conly—they were considered too young to attend most of the parties. A matter of regret to none of them except Rosie Travilla and Lucilla Raymond, and even they, though they would have been glad to be permitted to go, made no remonstrance or complaint but submitted cheerfully to the decision of their elders.

A busy, happy winter and spring followed, bringing no unusual event to any branch of the family.

Max was frequently heard from, and his father continued to send him daily letters, several of which would be replied to together by one from the lad—always frank, candid, and affectionate, sometimes expressing great longing for a sight of home and the dear ones there.

After receiving such a letter, the captain was very apt to pay a flying visit to the Academy in the case there was no special reasons for remaining closely at home. Sometimes he went alone, at others taking one or more members of the family with him—either his wife, if she could make it convenient to go, or one or more of his daughters, by whom the little trip and the sight of their brother were esteemed a great reward for good conduct and perfect recitations.

Both they and the lad himself looked forward with ardent desire and joyous anticipation to the June commencement, after which would begin the one long holiday Max would have during the six years of his course at the Academy.

The holidays for the home pupils began a day or two earlier, and a merry party, including, besides the captain and his immediate family, the rest of his pupils, Grandma Elsie, and her father and his wife boarded the *Dolphin* and set sail for Annapolis to attend the commencement at the Naval Academy.

The weather was delightful, and all greatly enjoyed the little trip. On their arrival they found Max well and in fine spirits. The reports of both his studies and conduct were all that could be desired, and the home friends—his father especially—regarded him with both pride and affection, and all expressed much pleasure in the fact that he was to accompany them on the return trip.

Max dearly loved his home, and during the nearly two years of his absence from Woodburn, he had had occasional fits of excessive homesickness. He longed more, however, for the dear ones dwelling there than for the place. So, he was full of joy on learning that everyone of the family was on board the *Dolphin*.

No one cared to tarry long at Annapolis, and they set out on the return trip as soon as Max was free to go with them.

The lovely weather continued. There was nothing to mar the pleasure of the short voyage, or the drive and ride that succeeded it. The carriages and Max's pony, Rex, which he hailed with almost a shout of delight and hastened to mount, were found awaiting them at the wharf to take them to their respective homes, Ion and Woodburn, which each seemed to the young cadet to be looking even more beautiful than ever before.

"Oh, was there ever a lovelier place?" was his delighted exclamation as the carriage, closely followed by Rex, turned in at the great gates giving admission to the Woodburn driveway. "I thought that of it before I left, but it is vastly improved—almost an earthly paradise."

"So I think," said Violet. "It does credit to your father's taste."

"And yours," added her husband with a pleased smile. "Have I not always consulted with my wife before making any alteration or adding what I thought would be an improvement? And has not the first suggestion come from her on more than one occasion?"

"Quite true," she returned, giving him a look of loving appreciation. "In fact, my dear, you are so ready to humor and indulge me in every possible way that I am half afraid to make a suggestion."

"Lest I should have too much pleasure in carrying it out?" he queried with playful look and tone.

"Oh, certainly!" she replied with a musical laugh. "It would be a sad pity to spoil so good a husband."

"Father, may I ride over the grounds before alighting?" asked Max's voice in eager tones, just at that moment.

"If you wish, my son," the captain answered pleasantly. "But suppose you delay a little and let some of us accompany you?"

"Yes, sir. That will be better," was the prompt, cheerful rejoinder, and in another minute Max had dismounted at the door of the mansion and stood ready to assist the occupants of the carriage to alight from it.

"Ah, I see you have been making some changes and improvements here, father," he said, glancing about as he entered the hall door.

"Yes, and in other parts of the house," said Violet. "Perhaps you might as well go over it before visiting the grounds."

"I am at liberty to go everywhere, as of old?" he returned, half in assertion, half inquiringly, turning from her to his father.

"Certainly, my son. It is as truly your father's house, therefore open in every part to you, as it was before you left its shelter for Uncle Sam's Naval Academy," replied the captain, regarding the lad with mingled fatherly affection, pride, and amusement.

"Thank you, sir," returned Max heartily. "Ah, Christine!" as the housekeeper, whom something had detained in another part of the house at the moment of their arrival, now appeared among them, "I'm pleased to see you again. You are looking so well, too. I really don't think you have changed in the least in all the time I have been away," shaking her hand warmly as he spoke.

"Ah, Master Max, sir, I can't say the same of you," she returned with a pleasant smile into the bright, young face. "You are growing up fast and looking more than ever like your father."

"Thank you," laughed Max, his eyes shining. "You could not ever possibly give me a higher compliment than that, Christine."

"Ah, who can say that I am not the complimented one, Max?" laughed the captain.

"I, papa," cried Lulu. "Oh, Maxie, come upstairs and see the improvements there. You can look at the downstairs rooms and grounds afterward."

"Yes, run along, children," said their father. "And make yourselves ready for the tea table before you come down again."

"Yes, sir," they answered in cheerful tones, Max catching up little Ned as he spoke and setting him on his shoulder. "Hold on tight, laddie, and your big brother will carry you up," he said. One chubby arm instantly went round his neck and a gleeful laugh accompanying it as Max began the ascent, his sisters following, Violet and the captain presently bringing up the rear.

"Into our rooms first, Max," said Violet. "You, too, Lulu and Gracie, that you may hear what he has to say about things there."

"Thank you, Mamma Vi," returned Max. "I want to visit every room in the house and have all the family go with me if they like."

"You will find a few additions here and there to the furnishings, but no great changes anywhere, Max," said his father.

"I should hope not, sir, as things seemed to me pretty nearly perfect before I went away," returned Max in a lively tone. "I only wish everyone of my mates had as sweet a home to spend his long vacation in and as kind a father and friends to help him enjoy it."

"Ah, we may well pity the lad who lacks the blessings of a good home and affectionate parents," said the captain. "I can never forget how much they were to me in my boyhood."

"I think you must have forgotten how long I have been away, papa," laughed Max as they finished the circuit of the rooms on that floor. "I have come upon a good many new things."

"Ah, well, they have been added so gradually that I did not realize how numerous they were," returned his father. "Now you may as well go on to the upper rooms and tarry long enough in your own to make yourself neat for the tea table."

"Yes, sir," and the lad hurried up the stairs, the captain, Lulu, and Gracie following.

"Hurrah!" he cried joyously as he reached the open door of is own room. "Why, this is lovely! Prettier than ever, and it is like a room in a palace compared to the sparsely decorated one I share with Hunt at the Academy."

"Suppose you walk in and take a nearer view," said his father, and Max obeyed with alacrity, the others following.

"Mamma said there was nothing too good for you, and so we all thought, Maxie," said Gracie.

Lulu added, "Indeed we do all think so."

"Indeed, I'm afraid it is," returned Max, gazing admiringly at the beautiful carpet, the lace curtains looped back with wreaths of flowers, the fine engravings on the walls, the easy chairs, tasteful mantel ornaments, and the various articles of adornment and convenience.

"Your mamma and I have made some changes—improvements, as we thought," the captain said in gratified and affectionate tones. "I'm hoping you will be pleased with them, and as I look at you, I rather think you are."

"Pleased, papa? I'm delighted!" cried Max. "The only drawback to my pleasure is the thought of the very short time I can stay to enjoy all this beauty and luxury."

"I am sure my boy does not want to settle down here to a life of ignoble ease," remarked the captain in a tone of mingled assertion and inquiry. "I rejoice in the firm conviction that his great desire is to serve God and his country to the best of his ability."

"Yes, father, it is," said Max earnestly. "But," he added with a smile, "if you don't want me to love to be with you in this sweet home you should not make it so attractive and be so very kind and affectionate to me."

"My boy," the captain said with emotion, laying a hand affectionately on his son's shoulder, "there is never a day when I do not thank my heavenly Father for His precious gift to me of so good and dutiful a son."

"I don't know how any fellow could help being dutiful and affectionate to such a father as mine, sir," returned Max, his eyes shining.

By his own desire, Max's vacation was spent at home and in its vicinity with the occasional variety of a short voyage in his father's yacht, the *Dolphin,* which gave the lad opportunities for the display of the seafaring knowledge gained in the past two years, and he added to it from his father's store of the same under that father's instruction.

They were generally accompanied by the whole Woodburn family, always by Lulu and Gracie, Grandma Elsie, Rosie, Walter, and Evelyn Leland.

Thus the weeks flew by very enjoyably and on swift wings, and the time came for Max's return to Annapolis. So the *Dolphin* was headed for that port and presently steamed away again, leaving the lad behind with a rather sad heart at the thought that years must pass before he could again spend even a brief season under his father's roof.

Chapter Second

It is summer again, the summer of 1893, for two years have passed by for Elsie and her family. There have been few changes among our friends at Ion, Woodburn, and the other plantations belonging to the family connection, except such as time brings to all. The elder ones seem scarcely any older, but the younger ones are growing up. Elsie's sons, Harold and Herbert are now practicing physicians, still making their home at Ion but having an office in a neighboring village. Rosie has attained her twentieth year and entered society, but Walter is still one of Captain Raymond's pupils, as are Lulu and Gracie, now blooming girls of seventeen and fifteen, both their father's joy and pride. They, in turn, are as devotedly attached to him as ever.

Max is still a cadet at the Naval Academy, pursuing his course there in a manner altogether satisfactory to his father and friends. The captain thinks no man ever had a brighter, better son than his first born, or one more likely to do good service to his country in his chosen profession. It seems hard to him at times—a sad thing to have to do without his boy—yet, he never really regrets that Max made his choice of the naval service as his life work. He did, however, regret that Max would not be able to go to Chicago to visit the World's Fair, in which they were all much interested.

Some of the family connection had attended the dedication ceremonies of the previous autumn, and nearly all talked of going to the formal opening that was appointed for the first of May—among them Grandma Elsie, her father and his wife, and Captain Raymond and his wife and family. The captain's plan was to go by water—in his yacht—up along the coast to the Gulf of St. Lawrence, through that up the river of the same name, through Welland Canal and around Michigan by the Great Lakes to Chicago. He invited as many as his vessel could well accommodate including, of course, his wife's mother and grandparents to be his guests for the long trip.

Most of the younger gentlemen and their wives preferred going by rail as the speedier way. But Mr. Dinsmore, having no longer any business to attend to, and both he and his wife being fond of the sea and desirous of keeping with his eldest daughter, accepted the invitation promptly and with evident pleasure.

Mr. Ronald Lilburn, too, having a like taste as to his mode of travel and no business engagements to hurry him, availed himself of the opportunity to make the journey by water. The other passengers were Evelyn Leland and Rosie and Walter Travilla.

Something, however, occurred to change their plans, and it was the latter part of June when they left home for their trip to the North. They had a pleasant voyage, making few pauses by the way, and reached their destination on Monday, the second day of July.

It was early in the evening when the *Dolphin* neared the White City. The little ones were already in bed and sweetly sleeping, but all the others had gathered on deck to catch the first glimpse of the fairy-like scene. They had passed the mouth of the Chicago River and had steamed on down the lake.

"Oh, papa, what is that?" asked Gracie, pointing to a bright light in the water.

"A lighted buoy," he replied. "A spar buoy with an incandescent lamp of one hundred candle power. It is a wrought iron cage at the end of a spar that is held in place by a heavy cast iron anchor. You will see another presently, for there are thirteen between the river and the White City."

"To warn vessels to keep off the shoals, papa?" she asked.

"Yes," he said and went on to explain how the electrical current was supplied, winding up with a promise to take her, and anyone else who wished to go, to the Electrical Building to gaze upon the wonders and for a ride in the electric launches. "But," he added, "I think there is nothing you will enjoy more than the sight of the electric lights that you will get presently in the Peristyle and the Court of Honor."

"Oh, I am very, very eager to see it all, papa!" she exclaimed.

"As we all are," said Lulu.

"Well, my dears, I think we can all go there at once and spend an hour or two—all but the little ones, who can be left in the care of their nurse." He turned inquiringly toward his wife and her mother as he spoke.

"Oh, yes," said Violet. "They will not be likely to wake, and Agnes will take good care of them."

"I think we are all probably ready to accept your invitation with pleasure, captain," Elsie said. "Surely none of us are fatigued—unless it may be with lack of exercise."

"No, surely not," remarked Mr. Dinsmore. "And I, as well as Gracie, am eager to see the beauties of that much talked of Court of Honor."

"I think we will find some other objects worthy of our attention before we reach even the Peristyle," remarked Captain Raymond.

"Oh, look, papa!" exclaimed Lulu. "There is another of those lights."

"I am glad you brought us in the yacht, captain," said Evelyn. "This way, we can start out at once to see the sights—not being in the least fatigued with our long journey."

"And we have already a beautiful view of water and sky," remarked Grandma Elsie. "Those sunset clouds are certainly lovelier than any work of man's hand."

"Yes, mamma, and they are beautifully reflected in the water," said Violet.

"But such natural wonders can be seen at home," Rosie remarked in a sprightly tone. "I propose to give my particular attention to such as are to be found only in this part of the world at the present time."

"What will there be worth looking at before we reach the Peristyle?" asked Walter, apparently addressing his query to no one in particular.

It was Captain Raymond who replied, "I hope to be able to point out to you presently some exhibits worthy of your attention," he said.

"Oh, yes, the battleship *Illinois* for one, I suppose."

"Yes, she will come into sight presently, and we all will have an outside view of her. Some day, I hope to take all of you who may desire to go on board to have a look at her internal arrangements."

"You may count my name on that list, captain," said Mr. Lilburn. "I'm a bit too auld to take part in a fight, even in a righteous cause, but not for taking an interest in the means provided for ither folk."

"I want to see it, too, though I hardly expect to ever make one of the crew of such a vessel," said Walter.

"And we girls will want to visit her also," laughed Rosie. "Though I am very sure no one of us will ever form part of such a crew."

"Well, as my father has and my brother expects to, I shall be very much interested," said Gracie.

"Especially as we shall have a retired officer to explain everything to us," added Lulu with a smiling look up into her father's face.

He returned the smile then pointed southward, "Yonder it is," he said. "She is still too distant for a critical survey, but a better view will be afforded us presently as we pass it."

As he spoke, all eyes turned in that direction.

"Oh, what a big vessel she is!" exclaimed Gracie, as they drew near enough to obtain a good idea of her size.

"Yes," returned the captain. "She is a full-sized model, above the water line, of our Navy's coastline battleships *Oregon, Massachusetts,* and *Indiana.*"

"Not a real ship, papa?"

"No, only a model. She is built of brick on the bottom of the lake, and she merely simulates a real man-of-war."

"Only a model!" repeated Walter. "And how about her guns, sir? Are they real?"

"Some of them are wood, but there are enough genuine machines on board to destroy almost anything of ordinary resisting power within three miles range. But I expect to go more into particulars when we pay our contemplated visit."

"I suppose she must have cost a good deal?"

"One hundred thousand dollars."

"How much this World's Fair is costing!" remarked Evelyn. "Do you think it will pay, captain?"

"I hope so," he returned cheerfully. "What is worth doing at all is worth doing well."

They were drawing near their port, and there was much on both land and water to attract their attention. Presently they were in front of the beautiful Peristyle, gazing in awed admiration upon its grand Arch of Triumph, its notable colonnade and statuary, and catching glimpses here and there between its pillars of the beauties beyond.

It was impetuous Lulu who broke the silence with an exclamation of delighted admiration and an eager request that they might land at once and get a nearer view of the fairy scenes that lay before them on the farther side.

The other members of their party, old and young, seemed scarcely less eager, and in a very few moments they were all pacing that grand colonnade to and fro, and gazing out delightedly now upon the blue waters of the lake and anon upon the fairy scene—the Court of Honor—on the inner side. Soon they hurried their steps thitherward.

"Oh, there," cried Lulu, "is the statue of our great republic! Is she not magnificent?"

"She is, indeed!" replied Grandma Elsie. "See in one hand she holds a pole bearing a liberty cap, in the other a globe, an eagle with outstretched wings resting upon it. That symbolizes protection, which she has ever been ready to extend to the oppressed of all the earth."

"She is a large woman," remarked Walter. "As she should be to adequately represent our great country. Grandpa, do you know her size?"

"I saw it stated the other day," replied Mr. Dinsmore. Her face is fifteen feet long, her arms thirty-five, forefingers forty-five inches, and ten inches in diameter. Her cost was twenty-five thousand dollars, and the gilding alone amounted to fourteen hundred dollars. Quite an expensive dress for any lady, don't you think?"

"But we don't grudge it to her, papa," remarked Grandma Elsie pleasantly.

"No," he said, "nor anything else the liberty she represents has cost—in money or in life and limb."

"But what is her height, grandpa?" asked Rosie. "It should be very considerable with a face fifteen feet long."

"Sixty-five feet, and the pedestal on which she stands is thirty feet above the water. There is a stairway inside that you can climb one of these days if you wish."

All were gazing with great admiration and intense interest upon the beautiful statue, though seeing it somewhat dimly through the gathering shades of evening, when suddenly the electric lights blazed out from all sides, causing an exclamation of surprise and delight from everyone in the party and from others who witnessed the wonderful and inspiring sight. Words failed them to express their sense of the loveliness of the scene, as that mighty statue of the Republic dominated the eastern end of the lagoon. The grandly beautiful Macmonnie's Fountain dominated the other end, its Goddess of Liberty seated aloft in her chair on the deck of her bark, erect and beautiful, with her eight maiden gondoliers plying the oars at the sides, while old Father Time steered the vessel, his scythe fastened to the tiller. Fame as a trumpet herald stood on the prow with her trumpet in her hand, while the gushing waters below sported the tritons with their plunging horses, the terraced fountain still lower with its clouds of spray showing all the colors of the rainbow, as did that of the smaller ones to the right and left.

And what a ravishing sight was that of the Administration Building with its corona of light, its domes, arches, and angles outlined with those brilliant lights, as were those of the Peristyle also. The grand structures between—Manufactures, Electricity, and Arts on the north side, Machinery and Agriculture on the south—were so lit as well, and the beautiful fountains threw spray of all the colors of the rainbow.

"What a magnificent sight!" "How lovely!" "How beautiful!" exclaimed one and another as they moved slowly onward, gazing from side to side.

"Let us go into the Administration Building," said Mr. Dinsmore.

All were willing, and they sauntered on toward it, still gazing delightedly as they went.

Reaching its doorway, they paused for a few moments to look at the statue of Columbus. He was represented as landing with the Spanish flag in his hand. They listened to the inspiring music of the bands as they passed on into the interior, which they found as artistic and wondrously beautiful as the outside.

After feasting their eyes upon the lower part, they took an elevator—of which there were six in the building—and went up to the upper promenade, which they found also very beautiful, giving lovely views of the surrounding grounds. The vault of the dome was ornamented with allegorical paintings, some of the paintings commemorating Columbus's renowned discovery of America.

Looking out from the promenade under the dome, the saw the Ferris Wheel, upon which they gazed with a good deal of interest.

"I must have a ride in that," said Walter rather emphatically. "Mamma, you will go with me, will you not?"

"Is it quite safe?" she asked, looking from her father to the captain.

"Oh, yes," they both replied. Mr. Dinsmore added, "I think we will all want to have a go once if not oftener."

"Go where, grandpa?" asked a familiar voice, and turning quickly about, the group found Harold and Herbert close at hand.

Then there was an exchange of joyous greetings, and inquiries were made concerning some others of the family connection who had come by rail.

The answer was that some of the little ones were in bed at the hotel where boarding had been taken by the party, and they were in the charge of the faithful attendants brought from home, while the older ones were scattered about the Court of Honor and other portions of the Fair.

"We have been on the sharp lookout for you all," continued Harold. "And only a few minutes ago, we discovered the *Dolphin* lying at anchor down yonder on the lake. We had hoped you would be here sooner."

"Yes, we thought we should have been here weeks ago," replied his mother. "But as the delays were providential, we did not fret over them."

"If you had fretted, mother, it would have been truly surprising, as I never knew you to do so about anything," Herbert said, smiling affectionately into her eyes.

"No, that was never one of her faults," remarked Mr. Dinsmore.

"No, indeed!" exclaimed Rosie. "But Harold, can you take us to the others? I am sure it would be more pleasant for us all to be together."

"I cannot promise certainly," he replied. "But if we walk about the Court of Honor, we are bound to come across each other finally, no doubt, as they will presently discover the *Dolphin* and look about for you."

"Yes," returned his mother. "They will all surely know that we could not persuade ourselves to go farther tonight than this bewitchingly beautiful Court of Honor."

Even as she spoke, all were moving toward the elevator nearest them, and in a few moments they were again strolling along the shores of the lagoon, gazing with delighted eyes upon the fairylike scene—imposing buildings, playing fountains, the waters of the lagoon dancing in the moonbeams, and the pretty crafts gliding over them filled with excursionists whose merry voices and laughter mingled pleasantly with the music of the bands.

"Oh, this is just delightful, delightful!" exclaimed Lulu. "Father, dear, I hope you will let us stay a long, long while."

"I have not yet thought of fixing the time for departure," returned the captain. "And if our friends intend to go home in the *Dolphin*, as they came, there will be a number of voices entitled to vote on the question. My wife for one," glancing down fondly upon the beautiful, graceful lady on his arm.

"Thank you, my dear," returned Violet. "I for one certainly feel no desire to start for home any time soon, even as dear and lovely as I esteem it."

"Oh, here they are!" cried a familiar voice at that instant, and the two sets of relatives had found each other. Glad greetings and kind inquiries were exchanged, and then they broke up into little groups and sauntered on through the beautiful scene till it was time to seek their resting places for the night. After making some arrangements for the sightseeing of the next day at the Fair, they bade each other goodnight and hied to their places of temporary abode.

Chapter Third

"Oh, we have a lovely view from here!" remarked Lulu as they reached the *Dolphin's* deck. "I'm not at all sleepy, papa. Can't I sit here for a while?"

Gracie was saying, "Goodnight, papa."

He returned it with a fatherly caress, then answered Lulu's query.

"No, daughter. It is long past your usual hour for retiring, and as I want you to feel fresh and bright for tomorrow's pleasure, you, too, may bid me goodnight and go at once to your berth."

"Yes, sir. That will be best, I know," she said, rising promptly from the seat she had taken with a loving look up into his face, for he was close at her side now. "What a happy thing it is for me that I have such a kind, wise father to take care of me!"

"A father whose strong desire it certainly is to make you and all his children as happy as possible," he said, laying a hand on her head and looking fondly down into her eyes. "Now, goodnight, daughter, and don't hesitate to call me if anything should go wrong with you or Gracie."

"Am I also under orders to retire, sir?" asked Violet with a mischievous smile up into his face, as Lulu bade goodnight to the rest of the company and disappeared down the companionway.

"Not from me," he said, pleasantly taking a seat at her side as he spoke. "Have I not told you many times that my wife does what she pleases? At least, if she fails to do so it is in consequence of no order from me."

"No. You have never given me one yet, and I believe I should like you to do so for once that I may see how it feels," she added with a low, musical laugh, slipping her hand confidingly into his.

"Perhaps you might not find that particularly agreeable," he returned, pressing the little hand tenderly in his. "But just to satisfy you, I may try it one of these days. You are not disappointed in the Fair so far?"

"No, no, not in the least! Oh, how lovely it is! And what a beautiful view we have from here! How delighted our little Elsie and Ned will be with it tomorrow. I hardly know how to wait for the time to come when I can see and share their pleasure."

But now the others were saying goodnight and going down to their staterooms, and the captain remarked laughingly that he thought the longed-for time would seem to come sooner if he and she should follow their good example.

"So it will," returned Violet, promptly rising and slipping her hand into his arm.

She went first to her mother's stateroom, and the door being opened in response to her gentle rap, "Are you quite comfortable, mamma, dear?" she asked. "Is there anything I can do or furnish to make you more so?"

"I am perfectly comfortable, and I need nothing but a good night's rest, Vi, dear," was the smiling response. "Something that I want you to be taking as soon as possible. We find ourselves surrounded by so much that is wondrously enticing to look at, that I fear we will be tempted to neglect needed rest and so make ourselves ill."

"Ah, mamma, you and my husband are of one mind, as usual," laughed Violet, and then with a tenderly affectionate goodnight, they parted.

Both the captain and Lulu retained their old habit of early rising, and she joined him upon the deck the next morning just as the sun came peeping above the horizon.

Good morning, papa," she cried, running to him to put her arms about his neck and receive the usual morning caress. "Isn't this a lovely day? How we shall enjoy it at the fair—that loveliest Court of Honor is just like the loveliest of fairylands."

"With which my eldest daughter is quite familiar, of course," he returned with amused look and tone, smoothing her hair caressingly as he spoke.

"Well, I think I can begin to imagine now what a fairyland may be like," was her smiling rejoinder. "Papa, mayn't I keep close at your side, going wherever you go?"

"That is exactly what I want you to do," he said. "I should be troubled by losing sight of any one of my children, unless I was putting him or her in the care of someone whom I could implicitly trust."

"I don't want to be in the care of anyone else, papa," she hastened to say.

"But it will be quite impossible to see everything here that is well worth looking at," he said. "And our tastes may differ greatly in regard to the things we care to examine."

"Still I care most of all to be with you, papa. I'm not afraid of getting lost, because I could easily find my way back to the Peristyle and wait and watch there for you and the rest, but I want to share in your enjoyment and to have you share in mine," laying her rosy cheek against his shoulder and lifting to his eyes full of ardent affection.

"That is right, Lulu," he said, smiling, and patting her cheek.

"Ah, here comes your mamma, Gracie, and the little ones. You are early, my dear," to Violet as he handed her to a seat, took one at her side, drawing Gracie to his knee for a moment's fatherly caress. She then gave her place to the younger two, both eagerly waiting for their turn.

"Yes," Violet replied, "we are all ready for an early start for the Fair."

"As I expected," he said pleasantly. "I have ordered breakfast to be on the table an hour earlier than usual, and if our guests appear in season we will have prayers before eating, so that we may be able to start soon after leaving the table."

"Judging by some slight sounds I have heard, I think they are all up and will join us presently," said Violet.

"Yes, mamma, I do believe we are all in a great hurry to get to the Fair," remarked little Elsie. "Oh, papa, is that it over there where that arch is with all those pillars on each side of it?"

"And, oh, papa, what big ship is that?" cried Ned, catching sight of the *Illinois*. "I like ships, and I want to go there. Can't I?"

"I intend to take you there one of these days," his father answered.

Just then the rest of the party came trooping up from the cabin. Morning salutations were exchanged, family worship followed, and then breakfast, during which plans for the day were again discussed and further arrangements made.

They had scarcely left the table when Harold and Herbert appeared, bringing further plans and suggestions in regard to the sightseeing. They were anxious to help the newer arrivals—particularly their mother—to the greatest possible enjoyment of the day.

After some discussion, it was finally decided that they would go first to the Ferris Wheel, from which they would have a fine view of the whole extent of the White City. "Then to the Wooded Island, where we will probably find enough to keep us busy until dinner time," said Harold. "Perhaps even longer."

"No matter if it should," said his grandfather. "Since we are not hurried for time, we may as well let all get their fill of everything, and if some want to tarry longer than others, we can break up into smaller parties."

"Yes, sir. I rather think we will find that the better plan, as our party is so uncommonly large."

It was large, but they were congenial and greatly enjoyed being together, sharing the same pleasures of sight and sound.

In another half hour the entire party was on shore enjoying a second view of the lovely Peristyle and Court of Honor, through which they passed on their way to the Ferris Wheel. Their ride upon it they found so delightful that at the earnest solicitation of little Ned, they retained their seats during a second revolution. Then they left it and walked on to the Wooded Island.

"I want to take you to the Hunter's Cabin," said Harold. "See, yonder it is."

"What! That old log building?" exclaimed his sister Rosie, catching sight of it among the trees. "Who cares to look at such a thing as that?"

"I do," he returned lightly, "since it is a museum and memorial of Daniel Boone and Davy Crockett—two historical characters who were very interesting to me in my youth—and also gives one a very good idea of the manner of life of our Western pioneers forty or more years ago."

He led the way as he spoke, the others following. They found that the building consisted of one large room divided by a rope into two apartments, a public and a private one. There was a broad fireplace such as belonged to the dwellings of the pioneers of fifty or more years ago. There were beds and settees made of stretched skins, and skins of wild animals covered the floor. There were also tin dishes, candles, a stool made of a section of a log, and such cooking apparatus as was used in the kind of dwelling represented.

The cabin was occupied by a hunter who wore long hair and a wide-brimmed felt hat.

He was ready to answer questions, many of which were asked by the younger members of the party, who, as well as their elders, seemed much interested in this representation of pioneer life in the olden times.

"Where now?" asked Mr. Dinsmore as they left the Hunter's Cabin.

"I think Master Neddie here would enjoy a look at the ostriches," remarked Herbert with a smiling glance at the rosy, happy face of his nephew, who was trudging along with his hand in that of his father.

"Oh, yes!" cried the child in a tone of eager delight. "I should like to see them ever so much!"

"Then, if no one objects, that is where we will go," said Harold, and as the only rejoinders from the other members of the party were those of assent, he led the way.

"Is it a very expensive entertainment?" asked Walter soberly.

"Costs all of ten cents apiece," replied Herbert. "An enormous sum, but one cannot expect to see Old Abe, General Grant, Jim Blaine, and Grover Cleveland for just nothing at all."

"Oh, uncle!" cried little Elsie. "Are all those great men there? Oh, no, of course they can't be, 'cause some of them are dead. I know it was Mr. Lincoln they called 'Old Abe,' and that a wicked man shot him long ago. I also know that General Grant was sick and died."

"That is all true," returned her uncle. "But these fellows still wear their feathers, and they are very much alive."

"Oh, I know now," laughed the little girl. "You mean the ostrich man has named some of his birds after those famous men." They were now on the northern side of Midway Plaisance, and presently they reached the enclosure where the ostriches were. There were twenty-three, and all were full-grown and brought in from California. The sight was an interesting one to both the grown people and the children, and all listened attentively to the remarks of the exhibitor, delivered in solemn tones, in regard to the habits of the birds. He spoke of the male bird as most kind and self-forgetful in his treatment of his mate, or mates, saying it was he who built the nest and obtained the food. He also said that the male bird would sit on the eggs in the nest for sixteen hours at a stretch while the mother did the same for only eight hours. He had other things also to tell of the domineering of the female over the male, which caused some merriment among the ladies and girls of the party. This delighted the gentlemen, also, though they pretended to highly disapprove. All laughed together over the ridiculous movements of the flock in passing from one side of the grounds to another.

"What do they eat, papa?" asked Ned.

"Corn, grasses, seeds of various kinds," replied his father. "They swallow large stones, too, as smaller birds swallow sand to help grind up the food in the gizzard. Indeed, ostriches have been known to swallow bits of iron, shoes, copper coins, glass, bricks, and other things such as you would think no living creature would want to eat."

"They look very big and strong, papa," remarked the little boy, gazing at them with great interest.

"Yes. They are so strong that one can easily carry two men on his back."

"Is that what they are good for, papa?"

"That is one thing, and their feathers are very valuable. For that reason ostrich farms have been established for the raising of the birds, and they have proved very profitable."

"Don't folks eat ostriches, papa?" asked Elsie.

"Sometimes a young one, and their eggs are eaten, too. They are so large that each one is equal to two dozen ordinary hen's eggs. To cook one, they usually set it up on end over a fire, and having first broken a hole in the top, they stir it with a forked stick while it is cooking. The shells are very thick and strong, and the Africans use them for water vessels."

"Do they have nests to lay their eggs in, like our chickens?" asked Ned.

"They do not take the pains in building a nest that most other birds do," replied his father. "They merely scoop a hole in the sand. One male usually appropriates to himself from two to seven females, and each hen lays ten eggs—so it is supposed—all in the same nest, and each egg is stood up on end."

"It must be a big, big nest to hold them—such great big eggs as you say they are, papa!"

"Yes, and generally there are some to be found lying on the sand outside of the nest. Perhaps they were laid there by hens who came to lay in it but found another in possession—one who had got there before them."

"I have often heard or read that the ostrich leaves her eggs laying in the sand to be hatched by the heat of the sun," remarked Evelyn.

"Perhaps she does in those very hot countries," said the exhibitor. "But she cannot in California. Though, as I've been telling you, she makes the male do the most of the setting."

"Maybe that's because the eggs are all his but don't all belong to any of the females," laughed Walter.

"Perhaps that is it, sir," returned the man.

"Can they run very fast?" asked Neddie. "I should think they could with such great long legs."

"Yes," said his father. "The ostrich is supposed to be able to run at the rate of sixty miles an hour when it first sets out, but it is not able to keep up that rate of speed very long. It has a habit of running in a curve instead of a straight line. It is thus possible for men on horseback to meet it and get a shot at it."

"I think it's a great pity to shoot them when they are not even good to eat," remarked the little fellow in indignant tones. "Besides, they might save them to grow feathers."

"Yes," returned the exhibitor. "That's what we're raising them for in California."

"Papa, I'd like to have some," said Neddie as they walked away.

"Some what, son?"

"Ostriches, papa."

"About how many?"

"Couldn't we have an ostrich farm?" asked the little fellow after a moment's consideration of the question put before him.

"Well, not today, my son," returned his father with an amused look. "There will be plenty of time to talk it over before we are ready to go into the ostrich business."

Chapter Fourth

"I THINK THE LITTLE folks are getting tired," said Harold. "Yonder on the lagoon is a gondola waiting for passengers. Shall we take it?"

Everybody seemed pleased with the suggestion, and presently they were in the gondola gliding over the water. They found it both restful and enjoyable.

It was past noon when they stepped ashore again, and Ned announced that he was hungry and was wanting something to eat.

"You shall have it, my son," said his father.

"And suppose we go to the New England Cabin for it," suggested Grandma Elsie.

They did so and were served an excellent repast with handsome, young Puritan ladies in colonial costumes acting as waitresses.

After satisfying their appetites, they visited the other room of the cabin, which was fitted up as the living room of a family of the olden time. It had log walls, bare rafters overhead, a tall old-fashioned clock in a corner, a canoe cradle, a great spinning wheel on which the ladies, dressed like the women of the olden times, spun yarn, and gourds used for drinking vessels. Some of the ladies were knitting socks, some carding wool, while they talked together, after the fashion of the good, industrious dames of the olden time they represented.

All in the family connection, especially the young girls, were greatly interested and amused.

"Suppose we visit some of the State buildings now," said Mrs. Dinsmore, as they left the cabin.

"Pennsylvania's in particular, my dear wife?" returned her husband. "Well, it is a grand old State. We could hardly do better than to show these little great-grandchildren the famous old bell that proclaimed liberty to this land and all its inhabitants."

"So I think," she said. "Do not you agree with us, Captain Raymond?"

"I do, indeed," he replied. "My older ones have seen the bell, but I want to show it to Elsie and to little Ned."

"It won't hurt any of us to look again at that old relic of the Revolution," remarked Walter. "And, of course, we want to see the building."

So the whole party at once turned their steps in that direction.

Arrived in front of the building, they paused there and scanned the outside. All pronounced it quite handsome.

"Its front seems to be a fine reproduction of Independence Hall," remarked Mr. Dinsmore. "It has its entrances and tower."

"Yes," said his wife. "I like that and the quarter circling in those front corners—those balconies, too."

"Is that the state of Pennsylvania's coat-of-arms above the pediment over the front doors, papa?" asked Gracie.

"Yes," was the reply. "And the statues on the sides are those of Penn and Franklin."

Just at that moment two women, evidently from the country, came sauntering along and halted near the party.

"What building's that?" asked one of the other. "It's right nice lookin', isn't it?"

"Yes, and don't you see the name there up over the door?"

"Oh, yes, to be sure! Pennsylvany! Are ya goin' in, Elmiry?"

"Of course. That's the thing to do. Do you see? There's the old bell at the door there that they talk so much about. What they make such a fuss over it fur I don't know. It's ugly as can be and has a great crack in it, but it's quite the thing to talk about it and say you've seen it. So we must do like the rest."

"Yes, I suppose we must, though I don't see why anybody should, any more than you do," returned her companion. "It's ugly enough and certainly wouldn't bring first prize if 'twas put up for sale. But just see what handsome fellows those policemen are that's got charge of it! Enough sight better lookin' than it is."

With that the two went nearer, looked the old bell carefully over, then walked on into the building. While they talked, merry, mischievous glances had been exchanged among the young people.

"I wonder where they have lived all their days," laughed Walter, looking after them as they quickly disappeared through the doorway.

"I hope they are not Americans! I'm ashamed of them if they are!" exclaimed Lulu. "The very idea of such ignorance!"

"Descendants of Tories, perhaps," said Rosie, laughing. "Do you know its story, Elsie, that of the old bell, I mean?"

"Yes, indeed, Aunt Rosie! We've got a picture of it at home, and papa and mamma and Lu and Gracie have told me the story about it—how when those brave men had signed their names to that paper, it proclaimed 'liberty throughout all the land unto all the inhabitants thereof.' It rang out to let the people know they had done it. Oh, papa, please show me those words on it."

"Yes," the captain said. "Come nearer, and you can see and read them for yourself."

The little girl obeyed with alacrity, and when she had read the inscription, "Wasn't it very strange, papa," she said, "that those words were put on it when nobody even knew that it was going to proclaim liberty?"

"Yes, very strange indeed, and that proclamation has made it a very famous old bell."

"Is that the reason why they brought it here to the Fair, papa?"

"Yes, for many people will see it here who will never get to Philadelphia to look at it."

"I'm glad for them that they can see it," she said with satisfaction. "Do they ring it when it's at its home in Philadelphia, papa?"

"No, my child. That great crack you see has spoiled it for ringing, but it is highly valued and cherished for what it did in those days when our fathers had to risk everything to secure freedom for themselves and their children."

"They were good and brave men to do it. Weren't they, papa?"

"They were, indeed, and deserve to be kept in loving remembrance because of their brave deeds."

The rest of the party were standing near listening to the talk between the captain and his little girl and regarding the old bell with interest, though nearly all of them had seen it before. It was time for them to move on, for others were coming to view the old relic of Revolutionary days, and Mr. Dinsmore led the way into the interior of the building, the rest closely following.

They went all over it, finding much to admire, and Mrs. Dinsmore expressed herself as entirely satisfied with the building of her native state.

From there they went to the Woman's Building, hoping to find in it some, if not all, the relatives who had come with Harold and Herbert to the Fair. And they were not disappointed, for Zoe and Edward hastened to meet them immediately on their entrance and led them to the nursery, saying their little ones were there with their nurse. They intended leaving them in that pleasant place for a time, while they themselves would be going about from one building to another.

"Uncle Horace is here with his wife and children and the Lelands also with theirs," added Zoe, as she led the way to where were gathered the group of little folks from Ion and the vicinity.

Pleasant greetings were quickly exchanged, and the children were full of delight at the sight of their relatives, whom they had not seen on the previous day. Grandma Elsie was an especially welcome sight, for they all loved her dearly.

But time pressed—there was so much to see and do—and after viewing with approval and admiration the arrangements for the comfort of its young occupants, the older folk left that apartment for others in the building. They reconciled the little ones of their party to a temporary separation with the promise that on their return all should go aboard the *Dolphin* and have their supper there. The captain and Violet had given them all a cordial invitation to enjoy tea on board the *Dolphin*.

Taking with them those who were old enough to appreciate and enjoy the sight, they went into the Gymnasium, which they found furnished with every kind of machine and mechanical means for developing the muscles and increasing the strength of both boys and girls.

There were many children of both sexes engaged in the various exercises with evident enjoyment. The entire party, both older and younger, watched them for some time with interest.

Leaving there, they visited in turn the court of the Woman's Building, the main hall, the east vestibule, the library, the Cincinnati parlor, the nursing section, the scientific department, and, finally, the ethnological room.

All this took a good while, as there was so much to see, examine, and admire.

The ladies showed a deep interest in the various exhibits of needlework, the embroideries from Siam, table covers and rugs from Norway, the dolls dressed as brides, and the fine lacework and woodcarvings from Sweden. There was needlework from France, too, and there were large and very pretty vases from the same country.

Zoe was much interested in all of the dainty needlework for infant's clothes, the beautiful laces and ribbon flowers, and the famous paintings reproduced in silk.

They found Italian exhibits also, especially the laces of the queen—valued at one-hundred thousand dollars—worthy of particular attention. Yet, perhaps not more so than some from Mexico, including a lace-edged handkerchief crocheted out of pineapple fiber. There were also some very delicately beautiful woodcarvings, so delicate as to be called etchings.

There were embroideries and laces from other countries also—Austria, Spain, Belgium, Ceylon.

As they came near the exhibit from Germany, Lulu exclaimed in an undertone, "Oh, papa, what is that woman doing?"

"We will go nearer and see if we can find out," replied the captain. The woman sat at a table, and they found that she was making bent ironwork into candleholders, inkstands, hanging lamps, and much more. It was very interesting to watch her as she did so.

There was a good deal of leatherwork also in Germany's exhibit, shown in screens and tables.

But when they had all looked their fill they found it was nearly tea time. So they hurried back to the nursery, where they had left their little ones, and soon they were all on the *Dolphin*, where an excellent supper was awaiting them.

They were hungry enough to enjoy it greatly. Everyone was weary with the day's excitement and exertion. Poor Gracie—still far from strong, though perfectly healthy—so much so that by her father's advice, she went directly from the table to her bed.

The others sat for an hour or more upon the deck enjoying a friendly chat and a view of some of the beauties of both the lake and the Fair. All were about to bid goodnight and return with their little folks and nurses to their hotel.

"Wait a little," said the captain. "I am sorry but I cannot furnish comfortable lodgings for the night, but I can take you to the city and so shorten your journey by land to your hotel. I have ordered the steam gotten up, and we can start in another half hour."

His offer was received with hearty thanks, and the plan carried out to the great contentment of all concerned. The *Dolphin* then returned to her old anchorage on the lake.

Violet had gone down into the cabin to put her little ones in bed, and Lulu promptly seized the opportunity to take possession of the vacated seat by her father's side. He smiled and stroked her hair with a caressing hand. "I fear my little girl must be very tired with all of the standing, walking, and sightseeing of the day," he said.

"Pretty tired, papa, yet I should like to go back to that lovely Peristyle for an hour or two if you would let me."

"Not tonight, daughter. As soon as we have had prayers, you must go immediately to bed."

"Your father is wise, Lulu. I think we are all weary enough to obey such an order as that," remarked Mrs. Dinsmore.

"I found out years ago that papa always knows what is best for me," returned Lulu cheerfully. "Besides, he's so dear and kind that it is just a pleasure to be controlled by him," she added, laying her head against his shoulder and lifting to his eyes full of ardent affection.

"I agree with you, Lu," said Evelyn. "In all the years that he has been my teacher, I have always found that he knew what was best for me."

"Take care, girls, that you don't make my biggest and oldest brother conceited," laughed Rosie.

"There's not the least bit of danger. There is nothing could make papa that!" exclaimed Lulu rather indignantly.

"Hush, hush!" her father said, laying a finger on her lips. "Rosie does but jest, and your father is by no means sure to be proof against the evil effects of flattery than any other man."

"I think he is," said Rosie. "I was only jesting, Lu. So don't take my nonsense to heart."

"No, I will not, Rosie. I ought to have known you were but jesting, and I beg your pardon," Lulu said, and her father smiled approvingly upon her.

"Cousin Ronald," said Walter, "can't you make some fun for us tomorrow with your ventriloquism?"

"Oh, do, Cousin Ronald, do!" cried the girls in eager chorus.

"Well, well, bairns," returned the old gentleman good-humoredly. "I'll be on the lookout for an opportunity for so doing without harming or frightening anyone—unless there might be some rascal deserving of fright," he added with a low chuckle, as if enjoying the thought of discomfiting such an one as that.

"Which I don't believe there will be," said Walter. "For everybody I saw today looked the picture of good nature."

"Yes," said his mother. "And it is no wonder. The thought has come to me again and again, when gazing upon the beauties of that wonderful Court of Honor, especially at night when we have the added charm of the electric lights and the fountains in full play, if earthly scenes can be made so lovely, what must the glories of heaven be! Ah, it makes one long for the sight of them."

"Oh, mamma, don't, don't say that," murmured Rosie in low, tremulous tones, taking her mother's hand in a tender clasp. They were, as usual, sitting side by side. "We can't spare you yet."

"The longing is not likely to hasten my departure, dear," replied the sweet voice of her mother. "And I am well content to stay a while longer with my dear ones here if the will of God be so."

"Oh!" exclaimed Lulu, suddenly breaking the momentary silence. "Tomorrow is the Fourth—the glorious Fourth! I wonder what is going to be done here to celebrate it?"

"I presume it will be celebrated in much the usual way," replied Mr. Dinsmore. "Today's papers say there have been great preparations on the part of the Exposition officials and exhibitors, and that there are to be a number of patriotic addresses delivered in different parts of the grounds. Also there will be, without doubt, a great display of bunting, an abundance of firecrackers, the thunder of cannon, and so forth."

"And we, I suppose, will pass the day on shore doing our part in the business of celebrating our nation's birthday," remarked Rosie.

"Why, of course," said Walter. "Such patriotic Americans as we are would never, ever think of neglecting our duty in that line."

"No, certainly not," replied his mother with a smile. "We are all too patriotic not to do our full share to show our many foreign guests how we love this free land of ours and how highly we value our precious liberties."

"I propose," said the captain, "that we spend the day on shore, first consulting the morning papers as to where we will be likely to find the smallest crowd or the best speaker. After hearing the oration, we will doubtless find abundance of amusement in the Court of Honor and Midway Plaisance."

"And perhaps Cousin Ronald can and will make some fun for us," remarked Walter, giving the old gentleman a laughing, persuasive look.

"Ah, laddie, you must not expect or ask too much of your auld kinsman," returned Mr. Lilburn with a slight smile and a dubious shake of the head.

At that moment Violet rejoined them, the short evening service was held, and then all retired to their rest, leaving further discussion of the morrow's doings to be carried on in the morning.

Chapter Fifth

EVERYBODY WAS READY for an early start the next morning, and Harold and Herbert were waiting for them in the Peristyle. Some time was spent there and in the Court of Honor, then in the Midway Plaisance. Watching the crowds was very amusing—the wild people from Dahomey wearing American flags around their dusky thighs. The Turks, the Arabs, and men, women, and children of many other nations all wore their own particular costumes, so different from the dress of people in this land.

Then one-hundred thousand flags, very many American with their stripes and stars, and those of perhaps every other nation that had one to display were flung to the breeze, while bands from Cincinnati and Iowa, from Vienna, and Arabia had all got together and were playing *Yankee Doodle.*

There were, besides, many curious bands of Oriental musicians—some of them making great but futile efforts to play our national airs. They produced sounds that were by no means delightful to the American ear and were not half so pleasing as the sight of the multi-colored flags decorating the huts and castles of foreign architecture.

It turned out to be a day of pleasant surprises. As they neared the end of the Plaisance, they came suddenly and unexpectedly upon Chester and

Frank Dinsmore and Will Croly, the old college mate of Harold and Herbert, whom none of them had seen since the summer spent together on the New England coast several years before.

All were delighted. Cordial greetings on both sides were exchanged, and scarcely were these over when Grandma Elsie recognized a lady passing by with a little cry of joyous surprise. It was her old-time friend and cousin, Annis Keith.

"Annis! Oh, how very, very glad I am to see you!" she exclaimed.

"Elsie! My dear, dearest cousin!" cried Annis in return, as they grasped each other's hands and looked with ardent affection each into the other's eyes. "Oh, how delightful to have come upon you so quickly! I was wondering if I could ever find you in all this crowd and to have fairly stumbled upon you almost the first thing after leaving the cars is most fortunate."

"Yes. For us as well as you, Annis," Mr. Dinsmore said with a smile, offering his hand as he spoke. "Are you just from Pleasant Plains, my dear?"

"Yes, sir. We left there this morning, and but a moment since stepped off the train that brought us—nearly all the family of brothers and sisters with their children."

"Why, yes, to be sure, here are Mildred and the doctor and— Well, really Charley," shaking hands with Mildred and her husband, "I will have to be introduced to all these younger folks."

There was quite a crowd of them now—there were young, middle-aged, and elderly ones. As families have a tendency to do, they had been increasing in numbers, the younger ones growing in size, and all in years.

All wanted to be together for a time, and the older ones wanted to be able to talk freely about absent dear ones and other family matters. The younger ones were desirous to make acquaintance with each other.

"Suppose we take a car in the Ferris Wheel," suggested Harold Travilla. "Then, we can have a ride, a grand view of the Fair grounds, and a chat—all at one and the same time."

Everyone seemed to favor the proposition, and without further discussion they all started in the direction of the Ferris Wheel.

Arriving at the place, they climbed the broad stairway very much like the approach to an elevated station.

"This way, ladies and gentlemen," said a man in a blue coat, pointing to a doorway between two knotted beams, and they passed into a sunshiny room with two rows of chairs at each side. There were windows all about it barred with iron.

"This is one of the cars," remarked Captain Raymond in answer to an inquiring look from Annis, and he and the other gentlemen of the party busied themselves in seeing the ladies comfortably seated, then took possession of chairs themselves.

Other people were coming in, and in a very few moments the car was in motion, the click of the latch having told them they were being locked in.

Some of the party who were trying the wheel for the first time looked a trifle pale and alarmed as the movement began, and one or two of the girls asked low and tremulously if it were certainly quite safe.

"Yes, I am entirely sure of that," replied Harold with his pleasant smile. "But don't look out of the windows just yet."

"You are not at all frightened, I see," said Chester Dinsmore in a low tone to Lulu, having contrived to secure a seat close at her side.

"Oh, no, indeed!" she returned. "This is now my second trip, and I hardly felt at all timid even the first time, because my father had assured us it was perfectly safe. I have entire confidence in my father's opinion and his word."

"I don't know any man whose word or opinion I would be more ready to take," returned Chester, giving her a look that seemed to say he would be no less willing to pursue the captain's daughter were the opportunity afforded him. But Lucilla did not notice the look, for she was already gazing out of the window and thinking of nothing but the prospect from it.

"Oh, look, Chester!" she said eagerly. "This gives us such a grand view of the Plaisance. It is the second time our party have made this trip—no, not that—the second time we have been in these cars. We went round twice that day, and I hope we will go at least as often today. Presently, when we get to the highest part the people down below will look like the merest black dots and the houses like toy ones."

"Yes," he returned, "it is a trip worth taking. I should not have liked to miss it."

"Nor should I," said Lucilla. "I am thinking of asking papa to bring us here several times more."

"In that case, I hope I may be permitted to be one of the party every time, for it is a fine sight indeed."

"Are you and Frank new arrivals?" she asked.

"Yes, we got into the city last evening. We should have hunted up your party at once, but we did not know just where to look for you."

"We are making the yacht our home," she returned. "It is anchored for the greater part of the time at no great distance from the Peristyle. We spend our nights on it, but so far our days have been passed in visiting different parts of the Fair."

"And you haven't seen everything in it yet?" he queried laughingly.

"No, indeed! I heard someone estimate the other day that it would take more than forty years to do that, Chester."

"And in a few months the vast majority of the sights will be withdrawn," he said with a half sigh. "So we will have to content ourselves with seeing a few such things as interest us most. How long will you stay?"

"I don't know. That depends upon the decisions of the higher powers—in other words, of the older people. How long do you plan to stay?"

"Perhaps two or three weeks. It will depend probably upon how we enjoy ourselves."

"Then you will likely stay a good while, I think," she returned. "There! We are at the top of the wheel, and is not the view magnificent?"

They made the circuit a second time. Then seeing that very many people were awaiting an opportunity to fill their places in the car, they vacated them and wandered elsewhere about the Fair grounds for a little while.

Then Grandma Elsie expressed a desire to visit the building of her native state of Louisiana. She invited all in the party to go with her and take their dinner there as her guests. All accepted the invitation with apparent pleasure, and the entire party immediately turned their steps in that direction with obvious delight.

"Where is it?" someone asked, and Harold answered, "At the northern curve of the horseshoe formed by the state sites around the Fine Art Galleries and just west of the Missouri building. It is not a long walk."

"Ah," exclaimed Grandma Elsie when they caught sight of their destination, "see those trees in front laden with moss from our southern bayous! The sight almost carries one back to the old days at Viamede, doesn't it?"

"Yes, that and the foliage generally, which is of the tropical order," remarked her father in reply. "See, the cacti are conspicuous, and I do so like the simple style of the building with its galleries and verandas."

"And the site is a fine one," remarked the captain. "It is not far from the cable car entrance and fronting the Art Palace."

"Shall we dine first and then look at the exhibits?" asked Grandma Elsie. "I want to give you all a real southern dinner, hoping it may prove agreeable to your palates."

"I presume we can stand it for once, mother dear," returned Herbert, and the rest of the party seemed equally willing.

They passed in to eat and were presently regaling themselves with gumbo soup, opossum, and various other dishes peculiar to that part of the country represented by the building and its appurtenances, being served by cooks and waiters directly from the plantations of the river country.

Then, having satisfied their appetites, they spent some time in examining the exhibits in the building.

One of these was a picture of the Madonna by Raphael. There was also an exhibition of carvings done by women, which excited both admiration and surprise. In one of the rooms was some richly carved furniture from the state museum at Baton Rouge, which had once belonged to Governor Galvez.

They went next to the Florida building, which was a reproduction of Old Fort Marion, whose foundations were laid in 1620—the same year of the landing of the Pilgrims in Massachusetts.

The captain mentioned that fact, then asked, "Do you know, Gracie, how long it took for that fort to be built?"

"No, papa," she replied. "Can you tell us?"

"It took 150 years of toil by exiles, convicts, and slaves to construct the heavy walls, curtains, bastions, and towers of defense. Its bloodiest days were more than a century before our Civil War in which it did not take a very prominent part."

"Where are the curtains, papa?" asked little Elsie. "I don't see any."

"That is the name given to the part of the rampart that connects the flanks of the two bastions," replied her father.

"And it was also there that the Apaches were imprisoned," remarked Walter.

"Yes," returned his mother. "A most gloomy prison it must have proved to them, used as they were to free life of the mountains, prairies, and forests of their youth."

A little more time was spent in viewing all of the tropical plants and trees that adorned the exterior of the fort. Then they passed inside and examined the many beautiful things to be seen there.

Their next visit was to the headquarters of the state of Washington, where they were very much interested in the display of her native woods and the rockery built of native ores, showing pure streaks of gold and silver, thus illustrating the vast mineral wealth of the state.

"Where to next?" asked Mr. Dinsmore as they headed for the exit of the building.

"Papa, I'm so tired," little Elsie was saying at the same moment in a low aside to her father.

"I, too," added Ned, overhearing her. "Please, can't we take a ride now?"

"Surely," said Grandpa Dinsmore, overhearing the request. "I invite you all to try an electric boat on the lagoon."

No one seemed disposed to decline the invitation. Some time was spent on the water, then on the Intramural Railway. After that the whole party, at the invitation of Violet and the captain, went aboard the yacht, still lying in the lake at no great distance from the Peristyle, and partook of a supper that was no unpleasant contrast to the enjoyable dinner with which Grandma Elsie had provided them.

The little folk were ready for bed on leaving the table. The older ones rested for a time on the *Dolphin's* deck, chatting together while they enjoyed the sunset. Then they returned to the Court of Honor again to revel in its beauties under the bedazzling electric lights.

CHAPTER SIXTH

MORNING FOUND them all rested, refreshed, and eager to spend another day amid the beauties of the Fair. They started early, as on the previous day, found Harold and Herbert with their other young gentlemen friends waiting for them in the Peristyle, spent a little time enjoying its beauties and the never wearying view it afforded of the lake on the other side, and the Court of Honor on the other, then at earnest solicitation of the little ones they again entered an electric launch and glided swiftly along the quiet waters of the lagoon.

"Let us go now to the Transportation Building," proposed Rosie as they landed again. "I want to see that golden doorway, and I have not the least bit of objection to passing through it and examining things inside."

"As no one else has, I presume," replied her grandfather. "No doubt we shall find a great deal there worthy of examination."

"Yes, sir. Much more than we can attend to in one visit," replied Harold, leading the way, as everyone seemed well pleased to carry out Rosie's suggestion.

They had all heard and read of the very beautiful golden doorway and viewed it with keen interest and satisfaction.

"It is very, very beautiful," said Grandma Elsie. "A nest of arches covered with silver and gold."

"And that border is lovely, lovely!" exclaimed Rosie. "It contains such delicate tracery!"

"Papa, is it solid gold?" asked little Elsie, who was clinging to her father's hand on one side, while Ned had fast hold of the other.

"No, daughter," the captain replied. "It is not solid, though there is a good deal of both gold and silver covering the other and cheaper materials." Then he called her attention to a relief on the left side of the arch, showing an ox cart with its clumsy wheels dragging slowly along through heavy sand, while the travelers in it looked most uncomfortable.

"That, children," he said, "is the way people used to travel years ago when I was a little fellow, such as you are now, Neddie boy. And this—" going to the other side of the arch and pointing to the contrasting relief, "shows how we travel now. See, it is a section of a palace car. Some of the people are reading, others are gazing from its plate glass windows, and a porter serving some a luncheon."

"Yes, papa, that's the way we travel when we don't go in the *Dolphin* or in our carriage, and it's a great deal nicer than that ox cart," said Elsie.

"Oh, papa, there are some words up there!" exclaimed Ned, pointing up to a higher part of the arch. "Please read them."

"I will, son," replied the captain. "Though I think you are hardly old enough to fully understand them. This," pointing it out, "was written by Macaulay, of whom you will learn more about when you are older. 'Of all inventions, the alphabet and the printing press alone excepted, those inventions which abridge distance have done the most for civilization.' This other is by Lord Bacon. 'There are three things which make a nation great and prosperous: a fertile soil, busy workshops, and easy conveyance for men and goods from place to place.' Those words are put upon this building because in it are shown the different modes of travel in different countries—on the sea also—at different times."

They stood for some little time longer examining the details of that wondrously beautiful doorway, noticing the splendor of the arches and pylon, the stairways on each side, the roof of the pavilion, and all the other beauties.

"It is very beautiful and a great satisfaction to have seen it," remarked Mr. Dinsmore at length. "Perhaps it would be as well for us to go on into the inside of the building now, reserving further examination of this golden doorway for some future time."

With that he moved in, the others following.

Many of the exhibits there were more interesting to the older members of the party, especially the gentlemen, than to the ladies and younger people—locomotives and trains of cars such as were in use at different periods of time, showing the vast improvement in their construction since steam was first put to that use, models of vessels teaching the same lesson in regard to increased convenience, and comfort of travel upon the water.

"Oh, there is the *Victoria*—the most grand of battleships, sunk only the other day in collision with her sister ship, the *Camperdown*!" exclaimed Herbert. "See what a crowd of men and women are gazing upon it!"

"Oh, yes," said Rosie. "I remember reading a description of it in the papers just the other day. One of the English fleet's finest battleships, was she not, Captain Raymond?"

"Yes," said Captain Raymond, drawing near and examining the model with interest. "She was a grand vessel and the pride of the British navy. I should like to have seen her and am glad to have the opportunity to examine even a model. Ah, what a sad accident it was, especially considering that it sent to the bottom of the sea her entire crew of four hundred men and officers!"

"Oh, it was dreadful, dreadful!" said Gracie in tearful tones. "Especially because they had no time to think and prepare for death."

"Yes, that is the saddest part of all," sighed Grandma Elsie.

These friends presently moved on, and all, from Grandpa Dinsmore down to little Ned, found many objects that interested them greatly. But the most attractive thing of all to the young folks—because of the story connected with it—was Grace Darling's boat. It was the captain who pointed it out to his children.

"Who was she, papa? And what did they put her boat here for?" asked little Elsie.

"She was the brave daughter of William Darling, the lighthouse keeper on Longstone, one of the Farne Islands."

"Where are they, papa?"

"There are in the North Sea, on the coast of Northumberland, the most northern county of England. They form a group of seventeen islets and rocks, some of them so small and low lying as to be covered with water and not visible except when the tide is low. The passage between them is very, very dangerous in rough weather.

"Two of the islands each have a lighthouse, and it was in one of those that Grace Darling and her father lived.

"In 1838, a vessel called the *Forfarshire* was wrecked among these islands. William Darling, from his lighthouse, saw it lying broken on the rocks, and sixty-three persons on it in danger of drowning. His daughter, Grace, a girl of twenty-two, begged him to go and try to rescue them. It was a very dangerous thing to attempt, but he did it, she going with him.

"Both father and daughter were very strong and skillful, and by exerting themselves to the utmost they succeeded in saving nine of the poor wretched creatures who were crouched on the rocks in momentary expectation of being washed off by the raging waves and drowned. They bore them safely to Longstone."

"And that event made Grace Darling famous," remarked Lulu.

"Yes," said her father. "Many people, many of the great and wealthy, went to see the brave girl who had risked her own life to save others, and they heaped upon her money and valuable presents, so that she was no longer poor. But she did not live long to enjoy the good things bestowed upon her. She died of consumption about four years after her famous adventure."

"What a pity, papa! Wasn't it?"

"For those who loved her, yes, but not for her, if she was ready for heaven. Do you think it was?"

"No, sir, 'cause it is the happy land where Jesus is, and nobody is ever sick or sorry or in pain. But I don't want to go there yet. I'd rather stay a good while longer here with you and mamma."

"I want you to, darling, if such be God's will," he returned low and tenderly, bending down to press a fatherly kiss on her round, rosy cheek. "Your father would hardly know how to do without his little Elsie."

She looked up into his face with shining eyes. "We love each other, don't we, papa?" she said with satisfaction. "Mamma, too, and brothers and sisters, and grandma, and—oh, all the folks."

"Where now?" asked Grandma Elsie as they left the Transportation Building.

"I want to show you the German castle," answered Harold. "It is here on the Midway Plaisance, and it is a reproduction of a castle of the middle centuries. It is viewed by most people who have read of moat-surrounded castles with great curiosity and interest."

"There is a German village connected with it, is there not?" she asked.

"There is, mamma, and I think you will all enjoy looking at both it and the castle."

"Oh, I am very sure we shall find it is a faithful reproduction of the old castles of feudal times that we have read of!" exclaimed Rosie.

"It is said to be accurate," returned Harold. "And it is considered very curious and interesting."

"Is there a moat about the castle, Uncle Harold?" asked Gracie.

"Yes, and a drawbridge and portcullis."

"Oh, what is that?" asked little Elsie.

"A framework of timbers crossing each other, pointed on the lower edge with iron, and hung by chains in grooves in the chief gateway of the castle, so that on the sudden appearance of an enemy it could be let down to keep him out more quickly than the drawbridge could be raised to prevent his crossing the moat, or the gates shut."

"And what is a moat?"

"A ditch or canal. But you shall see one presently, and a portcullis also."

"Oh, I'm so glad we came here to the White City!" cried Elsie, skipping along by her father's side. "It's so very lovely, and there are so many curious things to see."

"Yes, it is a pleasant way of gaining knowledge. It is more pleasant than learning lessons and reciting them to papa. Is it not, my little daughter?" asked the captain, smiling down into the bright, little face.

"Yes, sir. But that's not a hard way, either, 'cause my papa is so kind, and he loves me and makes the lessons easy."

They soon reached the castle, crossed the moat by the drawbridge, passed through the arched gateway under the portcullis, and the young folks and the older ones also, gazed at it with much curiosity. They entered a spacious hall, the walls of which were hung with bows, ancient weapons, and armor such as was worn by the warriors of feudal times.

From the hall was an entrance to a museum where were shown many interesting articles as having belonged to those old times when the homes of knights and barons were such castles as this.

When they had looked their fill at all these, they left the castle for the village surrounding it, which consisted of reproductions of very old German houses with small porticos and sharp gables.

These covered three or four acres of ground and were built around a court, in the center of which was a music stand where a band of twenty musicians, in white uniforms and military caps, were almost constantly playing upon their instruments, making such delightful music that crowds of people flocked to hear them.

These friends enjoyed it greatly, and for a time they did nothing but stay there and listen while watching the players and the crowd.

But the children began to show obvious signs of weariness, and the captain, Violet, Grandma Elsie, and several others rose and moved on with them into a cottage which stood at the back part of the grounds surrounding the castle.

It was a picturesque-looking building, and there were a number of Germans in and about it, many of them evidently sightseers like these friends. It was furnished in truly German style with quaint old-fashioned mantels, holding old pieces of bric-a-brac, dishes, and cabinets hanging on the walls.

One room on the left as they entered seemed to be attracting particular attention, and they presently turned to it, paused an instant at the open door, then walked in, the captain and Violet with their two little ones leading the way.

The principal objects in the apartment were two wax figures, life size, representing a man and woman seated at a table apparently dining together.

They stood for a moment silently gazing, then Mr. Lilburn and Walter Travilla followed them into the room, hardly seeming to belong to their party.

Catching sight of the figures at the table, Walter nudged the old gentleman, gave him a significant laughing glance, then stepping forward, addressed the waxen man in a serious tone as though he thought him a living person.

"Excuse me, sir, but I am a stranger here and would like to ask a little information in regard to what may be seen that is really worth looking at."

At that there was a general laugh among the other spectators and an exchange of glances that seemed to say he must be either very blind or extremely simple.

Walter did not seem to notice, however, but went on. "Are the upper floors open to visitors, sir? And are there refreshments served there, or in any other part of the building?"

At that, the laugh among the people in the room and about the doorway grew louder—it seemed so good a joke that anyone should take those wax figures for living people. A burly German, taking pity on Walter's stupidity, said, "Mine frient, dose vos vax beobles, ha, ha! Dey don't can't say nodings."

With that the laughter grew louder, and another German, evidently good-naturedly desirous to relieve Walter's embarrassment, spoke, turning as he did so to the first speaker.

"Dat vasn't no sign de young shentlemans vas dumb. He can't help it. He t'ot dey vas life beoples."

"Nefer you mine dose silly fellows, young shentleman, dey doan' know noddings."

The words seemed to come from the lips of the waxen man, and the crowd was struck with great astonishment. "I would tell you vat you vants to know," he added, "but I bees von stranger in dese barts mineself."

Then the woman seemed to speak, "Come to de dable mine frient, and eat somedings mit us."

"Thank you very much," returned Walter. "You are most kind and hospitable, but I cannot think of intruding upon your hospitality." And with a bow directed toward her and her spouse, he turned and left the room, the rest of his party following and leaving the little crowd of Germans gazing at each other and the waxen figures in wide-eyed and open-mouthed astonishment.

"Papa," complained little Ned as they left the German quarter, "I'm so tired and sleepy."

"Hungry, too, papa's boy, aren't you?" was the kindly inquiring rejoinder. "Well, papa will take you back to our floating home, and I will leave you there with your nurse to be fed and have a good, long nap. I think Elsie would like to go, too. Wouldn't you, daughter?"

The little girl gave a glad assent, and arranging with his wife and older daughters where to meet them on his return, the captain set off with the two little ones for the *Dolphin*.

Chapter Seventh

Captain Raymond was not gone very long, and on his return he found the others sitting quietly listening to the music of the German band. They were ready to go at his invitation and test the excellence of the fare to be obtained at the Woman's Building. "There are cafes at each end of the roof covered with Oriental awnings," he said. "Surely we may expect as good fare at any woman's establishment as anywhere else."

"I think we certainly should," said Rosie in a sprightly tone. "There must be a lovely view or views from the roof."

"Doubtless," returned the captain. "Though we visited the lower apartments of the building the other day, we did not go up to the roof. So, I think that a visit to it will have for us the charm of novelty."

"Yes," said Grandma Elsie. "Let us go by boat up the lagoon. Gracie looks as if she needed a rest from walking, and I must confess I should not object to a rest myself."

The words had scarcely left her lips, before Harold had signaled a boat, and the whole party was presently seated in it.

A short but delightful row brought them to the landing in front of the Woman's Building, and climbing the stone stairway that led up to the terrace, they passed through the triple-arched colonnade that led into the interior of the building and did not pause until they had reached one of the cafes, where they might rest their feet and also satisfy their appetites with the good things abundantly provided.

Those important matters duly attended to, some minutes were given to the enjoyment of the fine views to be obtained from the rooftop looking at the statues of Miss Rideout, representing Sacrifice, Charity, Virtue, and Wisdom. They then spent a short time over the exhibit in the lower part of the building, and there Captain Raymond and Lucilla met with a pleasant surprise in coming suddenly and unexpectedly upon Mr. Austin and his son Albert—the English gentleman whose acquaintance they had made in their visit to Minersville some years before.

The pleasure was evidently mutual, very hearty greetings were exchanged, and Captain Raymond introduced his accompanying friends. Mr. Austin introduced a daughter who was with him.

A few moments were spent in conversation, in the course of which an invitation was extended to the Austins to take supper upon the yacht that evening. They parted for a time, the Austins having an engagement to meet some friends in another part of the Fair.

"Shall we go now to the Electrical Building?" asked Captain Raymond, addressing his party, and receiving a hearty assent from all, he led the way.

They found much in that building to greatly interest them—great electric lenses used in lighthouses; the Edison electric column covered with five thousand electric globes; and many other wonderful things. It was a beautiful scene in the daytime, but far more gorgeous at night, as they readily perceived that it would be. So they decided to pay a second visit after the lighting up that evening. Still their present visit was so prolonged that on leaving they found it time to return to the yacht. They met the Austins again at the Peristyle and took them on board in the first boatload.

The guests were numerous, including all the cousins from Pleasant Plains, and the three young gentlemen friends—Chester and Frank Dinsmore and Will Croly. The meal to which they presently sat down, though Captain Raymond had called it supper, was an excellent dinner of several courses, enlivened by pleasant chat, and proved most enjoyable to the entire company.

At its conclusion they adjourned to the deck. A pleasant air was stirring, the sun drawing near his setting, the western sky glowing with brilliant hues, while the sounds of life on water and land came softly to the ear.

The young people formed one group, the older ones another, each conversing among themselves, mostly in rather subdued tones.

"You have hardly been in America ever since I saw you last?" Lucilla said inquiringly, addressing Albert Austin.

"Oh, no. We went home shortly after bidding you good-bye after our brief acquaintance in Minersville," he replied and then added, "and I presume you had nearly forgotten us?"

"No," she said. "We have spoken of you upon occasion—papa, Max, and I—and I certainly recognized your father the moment I saw him today. I recognized you also, though I am not sure that I should have done so had you been alone, for, of course, you have changed much more in appearance than he has."

"Not more than you have, Miss Raymond," he returned with a look of undisguised admiration. "Yet, I knew you instantly, though I saw you before I perceived that the captain made one of the company you were in."

"Indeed!" she said with a merry little laugh. "I am afraid I hoped I had grown and improved more than that would seem to imply."

"But you are still as proud as ever of being American and as proud of your Stripes and Stars?" he remarked inquiringly and with a noticebly amused smile.

"Yes, most emphatically, yes," she replied, lifting her eyes to the flag floating overhead. "I still think it the most beautiful banner ever flung to the breeze, Albert."

"And, I suppose, from its constant display here, there, and everywhere, that that must be the idea of Americans in general," remarked Miss Austin in a slightly sneering tone. "I must say I have—naturally, I suppose—a far greater admiration for England's flag, yet I should not want to see it so ostentatiously displayed on all occasions as yours is."

Lucilla colored but was silent, fearing she might speak too warmly in defense of her favorite banner should she attempt a reply. But Chester took it up.

"Miss Austin must remember," he said, speaking in calm, polite tones, "that ours is a very large country, to which immigrants from other lands are constantly flocking. They, as well as the ignorant among ourselves, need to have constantly kept before them the fact that we, though spread over so many states, form but one nation. Otherwise, our Union could not be maintained, and we must continually impress upon all our people that this one glorious nation is never to be separated into parts. The flag is the emblem of our Union—a symbol that is unmistakable—and so it is displayed as the chief glory of our nation. Therefore, we love it and cannot see too much of it."

Even as he spoke, the sun neared the horizon. All on the *Dolphin's* deck rose to their feet, and as he sank out of sight, the firing of a gun from the *Illinois* announced the fact, saluted the flag as, at that same moment, it came fluttering down from its lofty perch.

"Thank you for your informative explanation, Mr. Dinsmore," Miss Austin said pleasantly, as they resumed their seats. "It has given me an entirely new view of the matter, so that I now think you Americans are quite right in your devotion to your flag and your constant display of it. And this Fair," she went on, "is wonderful. The White City is a perfect fairyland, especially at night with its blaze of electrical lights and its many colored electric fountains."

"So we all think," said Harold Travilla. "Have you been in the Electric Building yet?"

"Not yet," she replied, and her brother added, "But we intend to go. The evening is the best time for a sight of its wonders, I presume?"

"Yes. We have planned to go tonight, and we would be glad to have you accompany us."

The invitation, overheard by the older people and cordially endorsed by the captain, was promptly accepted by the three Austins, and as the shades of evening began to fall, all but the little ones, already in their nests, returned to the shore and were presently in the Electrical Building, enjoying to the full its magical splendor.

Croly was devoting himself to Rosie Travilla, Frank Dinsmore endeavoring to make himself useful and entertaining to Gracie Raymond and Evelyn Leland, while his brother and Percy Landreth, Jr., vied with each other and Albert Austin in attentions to Lucilla, leaving Miss Austin to the charge of Harold and Herbert, who were careful to make sure that she should have no cause to feel herself in the least neglected.

They spent some time in viewing the marvels of the Electric Building, finding the lights giving it a truly magical splendor not perceptible by day. It seemed full of enchantment—a veritable hall of marvels. They were delighted and fascinated with the glories of the displays, and they lingered there longer than they had intended.

On leaving the building, the party broke up, the Austins bidding goodnight and going in one direction, Croly carrying Rosie off in another, and the Pleasant Plains people vanishing in still another.

"Will you take a boat ride with me, Lucilla?" asked Chester in a rather low aside.

"If the rest are going," she returned laughingly. "I'm such a baby that I cling to my father and don't want to go anywhere without him."

"You mean the captain does not allow it?" said Chester inquiringly and with a look of vexation.

"Oh," she laughed, "I'm not apt to ask for what I don't want, and I never want to be without my papa's companionship."

"Humph! I had really labored under the delusion that you were grown up."

"Does that mean you are ready to dispense with my father's society? In that case I don't mean to ever grow up," she returned with spirit.

"Well, really!" laughed Chester. "If I am not mistaken, my sisters considered themselves about grown up and altogether their own mistresses when they were no older that you are now. Though, to be sure, I don't profess to know your age exactly."

"Well, then, Chester, you may look at the record in the family Bible the next time you visit Woodburn, if you care to," Lucilla said with a careless little toss of her head. "You will find the date of my birth there in papa's handwriting, from which your knowledge of arithmetic will enable you to compute my present age."

"Thank you," he said laughingly but with a look of slight embarrassment. "I am entirely satisfied with the amount of knowledge I already possess on that subject."

"Ah, and what subject is that upon which you are so well informed, Chester?" queried Captain Raymond pleasantly, overhearing the last remark and turning toward the young couple.

"Your daughter's age, sir. I invited her to take a ride with me upon the lagoon in one of those electrical launches, but I find she is but a young thing and cannot leave her father."

"Ah?" laughed the captain. "Then suppose we all go together."

"Willingly, sir, if that will suit her better," answered Chester, turning inquiringly to Lucilla.

"I think nothing could be more pleasant to me, papa," she said, and the others being of like opinion were presently gliding over the waters of the lagoon intensely enjoying the swift, easy movement and the fairylike scenes through which they were passing.

CHAPTER EIGHTH

IT WAS LATE when at last all the *Dolphin's* passengers were gathered in. The party to which the Raymonds belonged were the first, the young men who had accompanied them in the electric launch bidding goodnight at the Peristyle, and all had retired to their respective staterooms before the coming of the others—all except the captain, who was pacing the deck while awaiting their arrival.

His thoughts seemed not altogether agreeable, for he walked with drooping head and downcast eyes and sighed rather heavily once or twice.

"Papa, dear, what is the matter? Oh, have I done anything to vex or trouble you?" asked Lucilla's voice close at his side.

"Why, daughter, are you there?" he exclaimed, turning toward her with a fatherly smile and taking her hand and drawing her into his arms, stroking her hair, patting her cheeks, and pressing a fond kiss upon her cheek. "No, I have no fault to find with my eldest daughter, and yet—" he paused, gazing searchingly and somewhat sadly into the bright, young face.

"Oh, papa, what is it?" she asked, putting her arms about his neck and gazing with ardent affection and questioning anxiety up into his eyes. "You looked at me so strangely two or three times tonight, and I so feared you were displeased with me that I could not go to my bed without first coming to ask you about it and get a kiss of forgiveness if I have displeased you in any way."

"No, daughter, you have not displeased me, but— Your father is so selfish," he sighed, "that he can scarce brook the thought that someone else may some day oust him from the first place in his dear child's heart."

"Oh, papa!" she exclaimed in half reproachful tones. "How can you be troubled with any such ideas as that? Don't you know that I love you ten thousand times better than anybody else in the whole wide world? I just love to belong to you, and I always shall," she added, laying her head on his shoulder and gazing with ardent affection up into his eyes. "Besides, I am only a little girl yet, as you've told me over and over again, and I must not think about beaux and lovers for at least five or six years to come. I'm sure I don't want to think of them at all so long as I have my own dear father to love and care for me."

"That is right," he said, holding her close. "I think I can say with truth that I love my dear daughter much too well ever to intentionally stand in the way of her happiness, but I feel sure that the best place for her for the next six or eight years at least, will be in her father's house, trusting in his great love and care."

"I haven't a doubt of it, father," she said, lifting loving, laughing eyes to his. "And really I don't believe Chester or anybody else cares half so much about me as you do or wants to get me away from you. I like right well to laugh and talk with him and the others just as I do with the girls, but I'm oh, so glad I belong to you. I will for years to come, if not always. Yes, I do hope it will be always, while we both live. And Gracie feels just the same. We had a little talk about it not very long ago, and we agreed that we could not bear to think the time would ever come when we would have to leave our dear father and the sweet home he has made for us to live with anybody else in the loveliest place that could possibly be imagined."

"That pleases me well," he said, his eyes shining. "Gracie is no less dear to me than you are, and so frail that I should be far from willing to resign the care of her to another. But now, dear child, it is high time you were resting in your bed. So give me another goodnight kiss and go at once."

"I will, papa, and are not you going, too? For I am sure you must be needing rest as well as I."

"Presently," he replied, glancing toward the pier. "I have been waiting to see the last of our party on board, and here they come."

Lucilla went to her bed a very happy girl, her heart full of love for her father and singing for joy in the thought of his love for her. She had a long dreamless sleep, but she awoke at her usual early hour and, when morning duties had been attended to, went noiselessly up to the deck where, as she had expected, the captain had preceded her by a moment or more. She ran to him to claim the usual morning caress.

"You look bright and well, dear child," he said, holding her close for a moment, then a little further off to gaze searchingly into the smiling, happy face.

"As I feel, father," she said, laying her head against his chest. "I went to sleep last night thinking of all you had been saying to me and feeling so glad of your dear love and that you want to keep me all your own for ever so long." Then she added with an arch look up into his face, "Don't you think, papa, it will be best for you to have me under your eye all the time wherever we go?"

"I am not afraid to trust you, my darling," he answered with a smile. "But, of course, I want you near me that I may take the very best care of you always and all the time."

"Well, then, I'll get and keep just as close to you as I can," she answered with a merry look and smile. "But, papa—"

"Well, daughter, what is it?" he asked, as she paused and hesitated as if fearful that he might be displeased with what she was about to say.

"I was just thinking—please don't be vexed with me—but wasn't Mamma Vi only nineteen when you married her?"

"Yes," he said with a slight smile. "Sometimes circumstances alter cases, and I have changed my views somewhat since then."

"Yes," she said reflectively. "She had no father, and it was you she married—you who know so well how to take care of both her and your daughters."

At that her father merely smiled again and patted her cheek, saying, "I am glad you are so content with my guardianship."

❧ ❧ ❧ ❧ ❧

He did not think it necessary to tell her of a talk he had had with Violet the night before, in which he had expressed his determination to keep his daughters single for some years to come—certainly not less than five or six—and his fear that Chester and one or two others had already begun to perceive their charms. He had told her that he feared that the young men might succeed all too soon in winning their affections, and in reply Violet had, with a very mirthful look, reminded him how young she herself was at the time of their marriage, and that he did not seem to think it at all necessary to wait for her to grow older.

In answer to that he had laughingly insisted that she was far more mature than his daughters bid fair to be at the same age, adding that he certainly ought to have gained something in wisdom in the years that had passed since their marriage.

"Ah," said Violet, giving him a look of ardent affection, "after all I am glad you had not attained to all that wisdom some years earlier, my dear husband. For my life with you has been such a happy, happy one. Your dear love is my greatest earthly treasure, and our little son and daughter scarcely less a joy of heart to me."

"To me also," he said, drawing her into his arms and giving her tenderest caresses. "Yet not quite so dear as their mother. For you, my love, have the very first place in my heart."

"And you in mine," she returned, her eyes dewy with happy tears. "I love your daughters dearly, dearly. I could hardly bear to part with them, and I am glad to perceive that they, as yet, care nothing for beaux. They seem entirely devoted to their father and happy in his love."

"Yes, I think they are, and I fondly hope they will continue to be for a number of years to come," was his pleased response.

"I have no doubt they will," said Violet, and there the conversation ended.

ꕥ ꕥ ꕥ ꕥ ꕥ

"I am more than content, papa. For as I have often said, I just delight in belonging to you," was Lucilla's glad response to his last remark in that morning talk.

"Yes, I know you do, and so we are a very happy father and daughter," he said. "I often think no man was ever more blessed in his children than I am in mine."

The talk about the breakfast table that morning was of the places it might be most desirable to visit that day, and the final conclusion that they would first go to the battleship *Illinois,* then to the lighthouse and life-saving station both near at hand.

"I am glad we are going aboard a battleship—or rather the model one, I presume I should say. Especially in the company with a naval officer who can explain everything to us," remarked Rosie in a lively tone.

"Yes, we are very fortunate in that," said Mrs. Dinsmore, giving Captain Raymond an appreciative look and smile."

"Papa, didn't you say she wasn't a real ship?" asked little Elsie, looking up inquiringly into her father's face.

"Yes, my child, but in all you could perceive in going aboard of her she is exactly like one. She is a facsimile of the coastline battleship *Illinois,* which is a very powerful vessel."

"And are her guns real, papa? Mightn't they go off and shoot us?"

"No, daughter, there is no danger of that. The largest ones are wooden models, and though quite a number are real and capable of firing, there is no danger of their being used on us."

"I'm not a bit afraid of them!" cried little Ned, straightening himself up with a very brave, defiant air. "Not with papa along, anyhow."

"No, you needn't be, Ned," laughed Walter. "For most assuredly nobody would dare to shoot Captain Raymond or anybody under his care."

"No, indeed, I should think not," chuckled the little fellow with a proudly affectionate look up into his father's face.

"No, nor any other visitor to the ship," said the captain. "We may go there without feeling the least apprehension of such a reception."

"So we will start for the *Illinois* as soon as we are ready for the day's pleasures," said Violet, smiling into the bright little face of her boy.

Harold and Herbert joined them at the usual early hour, bringing Chester and Frank Dinsmore with them, and in a few minutes they were all upon the deck of the model battleship.

They were treated very politely and shown every department from sleeping quarters to gun deck. They were told that she was steel armor-plated below the berth deck and were shown that above the decks were steel turrets, through portholes of which, deep-mouthed wooden guns projected. The group also found that she was fully manned and officered with a crew of two hundred men, who gave daily drills and performed all of the regular duties required of them when in actual service on the high sea.

From the battleship they went to the lighthouse and life-saving station.

On the plaza in front of the Government Building was the life-saving corps. It was neat and pretty, and close beside it was the model of a government lighthouse. Some of the party went to the top of that, and all of them viewed the paraphernalia used in the saving of life when a vessel is wrecked within sight of shore. Some of them had already seen it on the eastern shore, but they were sufficiently interested to care to look at it again, while to the others it was altogether new, as was the drill through which the company of life guards were presently put for both the benefit to themselves for the practice and the edification of visitors.

That over, Grandma Elsie asked, "Shall we not, now we are here, go into the Government Building and look at the military exhibit?"

"I should like to do so," said Mr. Dinsmore. "In what part of the building is it, Harold?"

"The southeastern, sir. I have been once and found many things worth looking at more than once."

Harold led the way as he spoke, the others of their party following closely.

The first department they entered contained exhibits of metal work, gun and cartridge making machines, campaign materials, and battleflags.

All were interesting to the gentlemen and to some of the ladies also, but to the others and the children the battleflags were far more so than anything else. It was the greatest collection ever seen outside of a government museum. They were mementos of all the wars our country had passed through since the settlement of Jamestown, Virginia.

There were also mountain howitzers mounted on mules, forage wagons, propeller torpedoes, and every kind of camp appliance, garrison equipage, packsaddles, and much more. Famous relics, too, such as a beautifully carved bronze cannon captured from the British at Yorktown in 1781, a great gun called "Long Tom," with which the privateer *General Armstrong* repelled a British squadron off the shores of the Azores in 1814, and many other souvenirs of American history.

"'Long Tom,'" repeated little Elsie, gazing quite curiously at the great gun, about which some remark had been made a moment before, "I s'pose there's a story to it. I wish somebody would tell it to Neddie and me."

"You shall hear it one of these times," said her father. "But not here and now," and with that she was content, for her papa's promises were sure to be kept.

"Don't refrain on my account from telling it here and now, captain," said Cousin Ronald with a humorous look and smile. "I'm not one to endorse wrong doing even on the part of the Britons."

"We are all sure of that, sir," returned the captain. "But this time and place are not the most favorable for the telling of a story of that length."

"And grandma will sit down somewhere with the children presently for a rest in some quiet place, and she can tell them the story of the gun should they wish to hear it," said Mrs. Travilla, and with that promise, the children seemed well content.

Chapter Ninth

By the middle of that afternoon Grandma Elsie, Gracie, and the little ones were all weary enough to be glad to return to the *Dolphin* for a good rest.

After a refreshing nap, Gracie and the children gathered about Mrs. Travilla and begged for the fulfillment of her promise to tell the story of "Long Tom," and she kindly complied.

"The *General Armstrong* was a privateer, and the fight I am now going to tell about was one of the most famous of the war of 1812–14," she said. "The vessel was commanded by Captain Samuel C. Reid, a native of Connecticut. He went to sea when only eleven years old and was a midshipman with Commodore Truxton. He was still a young man—only thirty—when the event of which we are talking occurred. That was on the twenty-sixth of September, 1814, in the harbor of Fayal—one of the Azores islands belonging to Portugal.

"While lying there at anchor, the *Armstrong* was attacked by a large British squadron. That was in flagrant violation of the laws of neutrality. Commodore Lloyd was the commander of the squadron. At eight o'clock in the evening, he sent four, large, well-armed launches—each manned by about forty men—to attack the American vessel.

"The moon shone brightly, and Captain Reid, who had noticed the movements of the British and suspected that their design was to attack him, was getting his vessel under the guns of the castle. Those guns and his own opened fire at almost the same instant and drove off the launches with very heavy losses."

"That means a great many men killed, grandma?" queried little Elsie.

"Yes, dear, a great many of the British. On our side there was one man killed, and a lieutenant was wounded. But that was not the end of the affair. At midnight, another attack was made with fourteen launches and about five hundred men.

"A terrible fight ensued, but at length the British were driven off with 120 killed and 180 wounded."

"That was a great many," commented the little girl. "Did they give it up, then, grandma?"

"No, at daybreak one of the British vessels, the *Carnation,* made another attempt. She began with heavy fire, but the gunners of the *Armstrong* fired shots at her so rapidly and so well-directed that she was soon so badly cut up that she hastened to get out of their range.

"In all this fighting, the British had lost over three hundred in killed and wounded, while only two Americans were killed and seven wounded. But the *Armstrong* was a good deal damaged, and Captain Reid saw that he could not stand another fight such as she had just gone through. So he directed his ship to be scuttled to prevent her from falling into the hands of the enemy."

"Scuttled? What's that, grandma?" asked Ned.

"Making holes in the bottom and sides of a vessel, so that the water can get in and sink her, is called 'scuttling.' It was done to prevent the British from taking possession of her. After our men had left her, however, they boarded and set her on fire."

"Grandma Elsie," said Gracie, "I think I remember reading that the victory of Reid's—or perhaps I should say resistance—had much to do with the saving of New Orleans."

"Yes, that British squadron was on its way to Jamaica, where British vessels were gathering for the expedition to move against and take New Orleans, and their object in attacking the *Armstrong* was to secure her for themselves and make her useful in that work. Had they succeeded in taking her, they would have reached New Orleans while it was utterly defenseless, General Jackson having not yet arrived there. But Reid, in his splendid defense of his vessel, so crippled those of the enemy that they did not reach Jamaica until fully ten days later than the time when the expedition was expected to set sail from there. The fleet awaited Lloyd, and the expedition was thus delayed until Jackson had reached the city and was making haste with arrangements for its defense."

"Yes, grandma, I've heard the story about that," said little Elsie. "The story about how the British tried to take that city, and General Jackson and his soldiers killed so very many of them and drove the rest away."

Neddie was looking very grave and thoughtful. "Isn't it wicked to kill folks, grandma?" he asked.

"Yes, dear, unless it is necessary to prevent them from killing or badly injury us or someone else. The British were abusing our poor sailors, and it was right for our government to fight them, because they would not stop it until they were forced to do so."

"But you haven't told about 'Long Tom,' yet, grandma," said Elsie. "That big gun, you know, that we saw today."

"Yes, it was one of those on the *Armstrong* with which Captain Reid defended his ship."

"Weren't the Americans glad when they heard about it, grandma? Didn't they praise Captain Reid?"

"Indeed, they did! And also made him many handsome presents. The state of New York thanked him and gave him a sword."

"Hadn't he afterward something to do with a change in our flag, Grandma Elsie?" asked Gracie.

"Yes, our flag at first bore thirteen stars and thirteen stripes, and as new states were admitted, another star and stripe were added for each one. But it was soon found that that practice was making the flag very large unless the stripes became narrower and narrower, while there was nothing to show what had been the original number of states. Captain Reid suggested the plan of retaining thirteen stripes to indicate the original number of states and the adding of a new star every time a new state was admitted, and Congress adopted that plan. He was certainly a talented man. He also invented and erected the signal telegraphs at the battery and the narrows."

"I'm proud of him, Grandma Elsie!" said Gracie, her face lighting up with enthusiasm. "His defense at Fayal against such overwhelming numbers was wonderful. And so was Jackson's at New Orleans. England was a great and powerful nation while ours was but small and weak, but we were in the right, fighting against dreadful wrongs done to our sailors. God helped us to drive away our haughty, powerful foe, and deliver our brave country from her unendurable oppression."

"Yes, dear, and to Him let us ever give all the glory and praise. Oh, may our nation always serve God and trust in Him! Then no foe shall ever prevail against her."

"I hope we do, grandma," said little Elsie. "On a quarter papa gave me the other day, I saw the words, 'In God we trust.'"

"Oh!" cried Ned at that moment. "The folks are coming! I see them there on the Peristyle—papa and mamma, Grandpa and Grandma Dinsmore, Lu, and the others."

"Yes, and the boat is waiting for them," added little Elsie. "And see, they are getting in."

"Oh, I am so glad," said Gracie. "Though they are earlier than usual."

"Yes," said Grandma Elsie. "I suppose because it is Saturday evening, and we are all so tired with going and sightseeing that we need to get early to bed and rest that we may not be too weary to enjoy the coming Sabbath day."

"I 'spect so," said Ned, running forward as his father and the others stepped upon the deck. "Papa," he asked, "did you come home soon to get ready to keep Sunday?"

"Yes," was the reply. "We all need a good rest that we may be able to enjoy God's holy day and spend it in His service."

"Where have you been since we left you, Lu?" asked Gracie, as her sister took a seat by her side.

"Papa took us to look at the Krupp gun," was the reply. "It is really something and weighs 248,000 pounds. Just think—124 tons! It was certainly a great undertaking to bring it all the way from Essen, Germany to Chicago. They told us that at Hamburg and at Baltimore great cranes were used—one of which could lift a sixty-five ton locomotive—to lift the gun to the trucks that were to carry it on the railroad. They had to put eight trucks under it, fastening two together, then the two pair together, and so on till they had eight all well fastened to each other, when they laid the gun on them and started it off.

"And think, Gracie, it takes half a ton of powder and costs 1,250 dollars to fire that great gun once. We saw the steel plate, sixteen inches thick, through which a twelve-inch shot had been fired. It had cracked the plate and thrown the upper corner half a yard away. I forgot to say the projectile alone from that gun weighs a ton and can go sixteen miles."

"Oh," cried Gracie. "That's just dreadful! I hope there will never be a war where such terrible guns will be used—never any more at all. I hope that very soon, as the Bible says, the people 'shall beat their swords into ploughshares, and their spears into pruning hooks; nation shall not lift up sword against nation, neither shall they learn war any more.'"

"Yes," said Grandma Elsie, overhearing her. "That will be a blessed time."

"Yes, indeed!" said Lucilla.

"Where else did you go?" asked Gracie.

"Oh, we have been promenading along the lake shore, sitting down now and then on the seats to watch the many boats of various sorts and sizes, our own among the rest, and now, here we are to stay for the night, I suppose. I must, at least, for papa has said so."

She looked smiling up into his face as she spoke, for he was standing by her side.

"I think that will be best for each of my children and hope that my dear, eldest daughter does not feel at all rebellious in regard to the matter," he said in his pleasant, fatherly way.

"No, indeed, papa!" she responded heartily. "Though the beautiful Court of Honor is so fascinating—especially at night—that if you had given me permission to go back there after tea I should have been very glad to do so."

"And I should take pleasure in allowing you that gratification if I thought it best and right."

"I don't doubt that in the least, papa, and I am very glad to have you to decide all such questions for me," she replied.

"Will we go over there to the Court of Honor, tomorrow, papa?" asked little Elsie.

"No, daughter, we must keep the Sabbath day holy, and if we go anywhere it will be to church."

"And if we don't, we'll have a meeting here on our own deck as we have on some other Sundays, won't we, papa?"

"Yes, and the Lord Jesus will be with us, for He has said, 'Where two or three are gathered together in my name, there am I in the midst of them.'"

"Oh, papa, I shall like to think of that—that the dear Lord Jesus is here with us—but I do wish I could see Him."

"I, too," said little Ned. "Please, papa, sit down now and let your baby boy sit on your knee a little while. You have been gone so long away from me."

"So long, dear papa's boy!" the captain repeated with a smile of fatherly affection into the bright, coaxing little face. Seating himself, he took his little fellow in his arms and hugged and kissed him to his heart's content. "Papa missed his dear, little boy," he said, "but I hoped he was having a good time here with dear grandma."

"Yes, papa, so I was. Grandma's ever so nice, but I want my papa and my mamma, too."

"That's right, darling! Mamma and papa would never know how to do without their dear, baby boy," Violet said, adding her caresses to those of his father, the captain having taken a seat close to her side.

"Nor me, either, mamma?" asked Elsie, drawing near, putting one hand into that of her mother, and laying the other on her father's knee. Her look and tone were a trifle wistful, as if she were fearful that she was less highly appreciated that her brother.

"No, indeed, dear child!" they replied, speaking together. "We love you just the same."

"Gracie, also," the captain added, turning toward her with a tenderly appreciative smile. "You were looking very weary, daughter, when you left us some hours ago. Are you feeling better now?"

"Yes, thank you, papa," she replied with a sweet, glad smile. "How careful of me you always are!"

"Yes," he returned. "One is apt to be careful of his choicest treasures."

"It is so delightful to be one of your treasures, you dear papa," she said, going to his side in response to an inviting gesture, as Neddie got down from his knee to run to the side of the vessel to look at a passing boat.

"And so delightful to have you for one," he said, drawing her to the seat Neddie had vacated. "Papa feels that he must be very careful to see that the strength and endurance of his feeble little girl are not overtaxed."

"Mamma, too," said Violet. "Dear child, I hope the rest of tonight, tomorrow, and the following night may entirely relieve your fatigue."

"Thank you, mamma, I hope and believe that it will," responded Gracie in cheerful tones. "We will go to church tomorrow, I suppose, papa?" turning inquiringly to him.

"Those of us who feel able and wish to," he replied. "I intend moving up on the lake to Chicago when you have all retired to your staterooms and to lie at anchor there until the Sabbath is past. We will have our Bible lesson as usual in the afternoon and a service on board in the evening."

"I am glad of that, papa," said Gracie. "I always greatly enjoy the lesson with you as my teacher."

Chapter Tenth

Most of the *Dolphin's* passengers went into the city to attend church the next morning, but Grandma Elsie and Gracie, not entirely recovered from their fatigue, remained behind with the little ones. They watched the departure of the others, then Elsie, taking a seat close at her grandma's side, asked for a Bible story. "I like it so much better to hear you or papa or mamma read or tell it than to have to read it for myself," she said.

"Yes, dear, and I always enjoy reading or telling those sweet stories to you," replied Mrs. Travilla, turning over the leaves of her Bible.

"Please read 'bout Jesus walking on the water, grandma," pleaded Neddie.

"Yes," she said. "Here in this chapter Mark tells about Jesus feeding the multitude—five thousand men—with five loaves and two fishes, making so much of that small quantity of food that they all ate and were filled, and there were twelve baskets full of fragments left. Then he constrained the disciples to get into the ship and go to the other side unto Bethsaida, while he sent away the people. Now, do you remember what he did after the disciples and the people were gone?"

"Went up into a mountain to pray," answered Elsie. "Grandma, why did He pray when He was God and could do everything?"

"We cannot fully understand it, dear, but He was both God and man and loved to talk with His Father, God."

"Yes, grandma, I love to talk to my father," said little Ned.

"So do I," said Elsie. "He is such a dear, kind papa, and we all love Him so much."

"That is right," grandma said with her sweet smile. "And I hope you sometimes thank God, our heavenly Father, for giving you such a good, kind papa."

"Yes, grandma. Yes, indeed!"

"Now listen while I read," she said, and began, "'And when even was come, the ship was in the midst of the sea, and He alone on the land. And He saw them toiling in rowing; for the wind was contrary unto them: and about the fourth watch of the night He cometh unto them, walking upon the sea, and would have passed by them. But when they saw Him walking upon the sea, they supposed it had been a spirit, and they cried out: For they all saw Him, and were troubled. And immediately He talked with them, and saith unto them, "Be of good cheer: it is I; be not afraid." And He went up unto them into the ship; and the wind ceased: and they were sore amazed in themselves beyond measure, and wondered. For they considered not the miracle of the loaves: for their heart was hardened.'"

"Oh, dear grandma, I don't want my heart to be hardened like that—so that I won't believe in Jesus and love and trust Him," Elsie said earnestly.

"No, dear child. Ask God very often not to let it ever be so hardened, but that He would give you a strong and abiding faith—faith that will never for an instant doubt his power or love. Remember He says, 'I love them that love me, and those that seek me early shall find me.'"

"Early in the morning, grandma?" asked Ned.

"Yes, dear, and early in life—while you are still a little child."

"How, grandma? What's the way to do it?"

"Perhaps you may sometimes want papa when you do not know exactly where he is, and you go about the house and grounds looking for him. That is seeking him, and when you have found papa, you say to him what you wish to say. But Jesus, being God, is everywhere. He sees you, hears all you say, and knows all your thoughts. So, if you speak to Him only in your heart He will know it—know all you want and listen to your prayer. For He is so good, so kind, so compassionate that He will not turn away from anyone who really prays and asks with all his heart to be cleansed from his sins and made truly good—such an one as will be pleasing in the sight of God."

"Yes, grandma," said Elsie. "That's what papa and mamma, too, have told Neddie and me many times, and I do ask God earnestly very often to give me a new heart and make me His own dear child. Grandma, papa often tells me he loves me very dearly, but that Jesus loves me still more."

"Yes, child, the Bible tells me so, and it is very sweet and comforting to think of. Jesus loves to have us carry our troubles to Him, and He feels for us in them all. He says, 'As one whom His mother comforteth, so will I comfort you; and ye shall be comforted.'"

"Mamma is such a dear comforter to us when we are in any trouble or suffering any pain," remarked little Elsie.

"Yes, your mamma loves you very dearly, but Jesus' love is still stronger. Now, I will read of another time when Jesus stilled the waves with a word. "'Now it came to pass on a certain day, the He went into a ship with His disciples: and He said unto them, let us go over unto the other side of the lake. And they launched forth. But as they sailed He fell asleep: and there came down a storm of wind on the lake; and they were filled with water, and were in jeopardy. And they came to Him, and awoke Him, saying, "Master, master, we perish." Then He arose, rebuked the wind, and the raging of the water: and they ceased, and there was a calm. And He said unto them, "Where is your faith?" And they being afraid wondered, saying one to another, "What manner of man is this! For He commandeth even the winds and water, and they obey Him."'"

"Nobody but God could do that," Neddie remarked, half in assertion, half inquiringly.

"No, dear child, it is only the voice of God the winds and the waters will obey—or the dead when summoned to come forth from their graves. Jesus is God, and He is able to save to the uttermost all that come unto God by Him. The Bible tells us so—the Bible which from beginning to end is God's own holy word. Listen to its closing words." And again she read aloud from the Bible in her hand.

"'I Jesus have sent mine angels to testify unto you these things in the churches. I am the root and the offspring of David, and the bright and morning star. And the Spirit and the bride say, "Come." And let him that is athirst come. And whosoever will, let him take the water of life freely. For I testify unto every man that heareth the words of the prophecy of this book. If any man shall add unto these things, God shall add unto him the plagues that are written in this book: And if any man shall take away from the words of the book of this prophecy, God shall take away his part out of the book of life, and out of the holy city, and from these things which are written in this book. He which testifieth these things saith, "Surely I come quickly:" Amen. Even so, come, Lord Jesus. The grace of our Lord Jesus Christ be with you all. Amen.'"

"Is it Jesus who says, 'Surely I come quickly,' grandma?" asked Elsie.

"Yes, dear. And He says to each one of us, 'Take ye heed, watch and pray: for ye know not when the time is. For the Son of man is as a man taking a far journey, who left his house, and gave authority to his servants, and to every man his work, and commanded the porter to watch. Watch ye therefore: for you know not when the master of the house cometh, at even, or at midnight, or at the cock-crowing, or in the morning: Lest coming suddenly he find you sleeping. And what I say unto you I say unto all, "Watch."'"

"Watch," repeated Neddie. "What for, grandma?"

"That we may be ready to meet Him with joy and our hearts full of love to Him and His cause, caring little for the things of earth but very much for things heavenly and divine, setting our affections on things above."

"Oh, there they come!" cried Neddie the next moment. "Papa and mamma and all the rest," and he ran to the side of the vessel to give them a joyous greeting as they presently stepped upon the deck. In the afternoon, the captain gathered his young people together for a Bible lesson, which all liked as he was sure to make it interesting and instructive. The subject was the miracle of Christ wrought in the healing of the paralytic as related in Mark 2:1–12. "'Seeing their faith?' How did they show their faith, Lucilla?" asked the captain.

"By their works, papa. I think that if they had not believed that Jesus could and would heal their friend they would hardly have taken the trouble to break up the roof that they might let him down before the Lord. And the paralytic, too, must have had faith in the power and willingness of Jesus to heal him or surely he would have objected to being moved so much—carried from his house along the street to the place where Jesus was, then up to the roof, and let down from there in his bed."

"Yes, he, too, surely must have had faith in the power and willingness of Christ to heal him and is included in the number of those spoken of as having faith. Let it never be forgotten that faith in Christ is necessary to salvation; for 'without faith it is impossible to please Him;' but, 'all things are possible to him that believeth.' 'Ye believe in God, believe also in me,' Jesus said to His disciples in His farewell talk with them the night before His crucifixion. If we would be saved we must have 'the righteousness of God which is by faith of Jesus Christ unto all and upon all them that believe.' None can be justified by works, 'for all have sinned and come short of the glory of God,' and if we are justified it must be 'freely by His grace through the redemption that is in Christ Jesus.' Ah, let us all pray as did the disciples, 'Lord, increase our faith.'"

"Why did Jesus say to the man 'Son, thy sins be forgiven thee,' papa?" asked little Elsie. "I thought it was to be cured of his sickness the man came."

"Yes, daughter, but sin is the cause of all sickness and disease. If man had not sinned there would never have been any sickness or pain, and there will be none in heaven where all are holy.

"And in pronouncing the man's sins forgiven Jesus asserted himself to be God. The Scribes sitting there understood it to be so and said in their hearts, 'Why doth this man thus speak blasphemies? Who can forgive sins but God only?' And Jesus knew their thoughts, for He asked, 'Why reason ye these things in your hearts?'"

"That He could see their thoughts I should think was another proof that He was God," remarked Walter. "And when that was followed by the instantaneous healing of the man, it seems to me wondrous strange that they were not convinced beyond the possibility of a doubt."

"The trouble with them was the same with that of many in these days," returned the captain. "Their hearts were more in the wrong than their heads, and they did not want to be convinced."

CHAPTER ELEVENTH

MONDAY MORNING found all on board the *Dolphin* feeling bright and ready to enjoy further examination of the wonders and beauties of the White City beside the lake. As usual, the question as to which of them should claim attention first came up for discussion at the breakfast table.

"I, for one, would extremely like to pay a visit to Buffalo Bill's Wild West Show," said Walter. "I think my little nephew and niece would enjoy it as well, and possibly older folks might find some amusement there also."

"Oh, what is it, Uncle Walter?" asked Ned eagerly. "I'd like to see some buffaloes."

"Well, so you will if we go," replied Walter. "For there's a herd of them to be seen there. It is outside the Exposition grounds, but it is worth going to see, I should think. There are rifle experts, bucking ponies, dancing dervishes, athletes, female riders, besides American, German, French, English, Cossack, Mexican, and Arabian cavalry—to say nothing of cowboys and other attractions too many to mention."

"Oh!" cried Ned. "I want to go. Can't I, papa?"

"All alone?" asked his father laughingly. "No, my son, I fear you are rather young for that."

"Oh, no, papa. I don't mean all alone. But won't you take mamma and Elsie and all the rest and me, too, papa?"

"Yes, if mamma and all the rest want to go."

"There are two hundred Indians there, Ned. Won't you be afraid of them?" asked Lucilla.

"No, Lu, not with our papa along to take care of us. If you're afraid, I s'pose you can stay on the *Dolphin* here till we come back."

"Thank you, Ned," she said laughingly. "But I believe I feel quite safe where papa is as you do. And I think I should like to see that show myself, though I'm neither a baby boy like you, nor a sixteen year old laddie like Walter."

"No, not a boy at all—a girl. I'm glad I was made a boy so I can grow up into a man like papa."

"Well, I'd rather be a woman like mamma and Grandma Elsie," said his sister. "But I'd like to see the buffaloes and all the rest of it. Can't we go, papa? Can't we?"

"I will go and take my little girl and boy," replied her father. "And we will be glad of the company of anyone else who feels inclined to go with us."

No one seemed disinclined, and finally all aboard decided to go.

They were all well entertained, and, when the exhibition was over, the group moved out upon the elevated platform at the entrance.

The crowd moved slowly, and as they stood awaiting an opportunity to descend to the street below, there arose a sudden cry of "Fire!" At the same instant, they perceived a flame creeping up within the center tower of the Cold Storage Building near at hand.

Scarcely was the cry raised before twenty-five brave and experienced firemen were on the scene and ascending to the platform of observation that had been built near the summit. The tower was built of pine wood and plaster, which had been dried by the sun without and hot sheet-iron chimneys within, so that it was a very dangerous place for anyone to venture into. Therefore, they hesitated and drew back, but their leader swore at them, calling them cowards. At once they climbed to the perilous place, but scarcely had they reached it when there was an explosion of gases. The roof heaved and fell in, carrying with it sixteen men down into a pit of gaseous flame, and a shriek of horror went up from the fifty thousand people who stood looking on unable to give the least assistance to the poor, perishing men.

The party from the *Dolphin* saw it all and were sick with horror. Gracie fainted, and but for the support of her father's arm quickly thrown about her, she would have fallen to the floor of the platform where they stood. He held her up, and with the help of Harold and Herbert, hastily pushed his way through the crowd.

"Lay her down as quickly as you can, captain!" exclaimed Harold. "It is important."

"Yes, I know," returned Captain Raymond, glancing down at the white, unconscious face of his precious burden.

But at that instant, Gracie's eyes opened, and looking up in a bewildered way into her father's eyes, she said, "Papa, I'm too heavy for you to carry," she said faintly.

"No, my darling, not at all," he replied. "There, Uncle Harold has summoned a boat, and we will take you back at once to our floating home."

"Am I sick? Did I faint, papa?" she asked. "Oh," with a burst of tears and sobs, "I remember now! Those poor, poor men! Papa, were they all killed?"

"Don't be so distressed, dear child," he said with emotion. "I think they must have been almost instantly suffocated by the gas, and they did not feel anything that followed."

"Your father is right," said Harold, close at her side. "Though it was a very dreadful thing for them to be sacrificed in that way and hurried into eternity without a moment's warning, they are not suffering pain of body now. We can only hope that with their last breath they cried to the God of all grace for pardon and salvation." As he concluded his sentence, the boat he had signaled was close at hand. The rest of their party came up at that moment, all embarked, and they were soon on board the *Dolphin*, where they remained for the rest of that day, feeling too much shocked over the dreadful catastrophe at the Storage Building to care to go anywhere else.

Poor, feeble Gracie was almost overwhelmed with pity and horror, weeping bitterly much of the time. The others, especially her father, did all in their power to comfort her with the hope that at least some of the killed were prepared for heaven and with plans for giving aid and consolation to their bereaved wives, children, and other relatives who had been dependent upon their exertions for support.

The next day brought the very pleasant surprise of the arrival among them of their cousin, Dr. Conly, with his wife and her brother, Sandy McAlpine. The sight of her old physician and Marian, of whom she was very fond, did much to restore Gracie to her usual spirits, and all went together to view various interesting exhibits.

The first they gave their attention to was that of the relics of the cliff dwellers. It was in the southeastern part of the grounds and was a reproduction of Battle Rock Mountain, Colorado. As they neared it, they seemed to see before them a cliff, for though built of timbers, iron, stone, staff, and boards, it wore the appearance of rock and earth. There was a cavernous opening that had the effect of a canyon, and in niches high up were the dwellings, in miniature, of the ancient people who once lived among the tablelands of the southwestern territories. Portions of the real houses were shown in order to give a perfectly truthful impression to visitors. There were also relics of the old cliff dwellers shown, such as weapons wrought from bones, stone, and wood as well as pottery and cloths and mattings woven from blades of the alfalfa plant.

There were to be seen also ledges of fallen rock with houses crushed beneath and other houses built over them. Also, winding paths led up the cliffs and through to the outer air. The group climbed up these trails to the summit, where they stood for a little enjoying the prospect now on this side, now on that.

"Papa," asked little Elsie, "how long ago did these people live in those houses so high up among the rocks?"

"Nobody knows just how long ago, my child," he replied, "but probably hundreds of years before Columbus discovered America."

The rest of the day was spent in the Midway Plaisance—a street three-hundred-feet wide, beginning at the rear of the Woman's Building, extending about a mile in length, and so full of interesting sights that one might tarry there many hours. One could go again day after day without wearying of them but always finding something by which to be greatly entertained.

"A good and most entertaining place for the study of mankind," as Mr. Dinsmore remarked.

As they entered it, the sound of the sweetly piercing music of a bagpipe smote upon their ears. "Ah," exclaimed Mr. Lilburn, "that sound is sweetly homelike to my ear. Let us see, my friends, to what sight it summons us."

"The Beauty Show, sir," said Herbert. "Probably you have all heard of it—some thirty or forty belles collected from different parts of the world and dressed in their national costumes."

They went in, passing the handsome Highlander playing the bagpipes at the door. They found the women who were on exhibition ranged in pens around a large room.

"Beauties!" sniffed Rosie as she glanced about upon them. "There is scarcely one who I should have selected as such."

"Hush, hush, Rosie!" said her mother warningly. "Some of them may understand English, and surely you would be sorry to hurt their feelings."

"Yes, I should indeed, mamma," she returned in a regretful tone.

"The countryman of yours playing the bagpipes has the handsomest face about that establishment, Cousin Ronald," remarked Lucilla with a smile, as they proceeded on their way.

"I agree with you in that opinion, lassie," laughed the old gentleman. "And I have no doubt that he would also, had he heard you express it."

"How very much there is to see here!" remarked Dr. Conly. "There are men, women, and children from all parts of the world clad in their own native attire—Chinese, Japanese, Dahomeyans, Nubians, Arabs, Persians, Soudanese, Algerians, Javanese, and Cingalese."

"And some of the buildings are as singular in appearance as the people who occupy them," added his wife.

"Let us visit the village and castle of Blarney," said Rosie.

"You want to kiss the Blarney Stone, do you?" asked Herbert laughingly.

"No, none of that," said Walter. "She can blarney fast enough if she wants to, and that without ever having seen the stone."

"What is blarney, papa?" asked little Elsie.

"Coaxing, wheedling, and flattering," he replied. "The village we are going to see is said to be a fair representation of the one of that name in Ireland, about four miles from the city of Cork, in which there is a castle called Blarney Castle, which has stood there for more than four hundred years. The castle has a tower, as you will see, and on top of it is a stone the kissing of which is said to confer the gift of ability to wheedle and flatter. But the true stone is said to be another in a wall where it can be kissed only by a person held over the parapet."

"Oh, I shouldn't like that at all, papa!" Elsie exclaimed. "I'd be afraid of falling, and I shouldn't like to kiss a dirty stone, anyhow."

"Well, daughter, I shall never ask you to do so," he answered with a kindly smile down into the bright, rosy, little face.

They were entering the village as he spoke. Some little time was spent there very agreeably, after which they returned to the *Dolphin* for the night.

Chapter Twelfth

THERE WAS A GRAND gathering of friends and relatives on the *Dolphin* that evening—all from Pleasant Plains were there, Chester and Frank Dinsmore also, and the Ion family. The brother and sister of Grandma Elsie and her eldest daughter with her husband and children had paid their visit to the Fair at an earlier date and returned home.

Expecting to do a good deal of entertaining, Captain Raymond had taken care to have his boat well provisioned, and all were cordially invited to stay and take dinner on board.

No one declined, and they were a pleasant lively party, each having something interesting to tell of the experiences of the day, all agreeing that the Fair was well worth the trouble and expense of the journey to reach it, and the hundred and one demands upon the purse while there. Gracie alone was very quiet, seeming to have little or nothing to say and looking at times both sad and distressed. Her father noticed it and, seizing the first opportunity to speak with her in private, asked in tenderly solicitous tones if she were feeling perfectly well, adding, "I fear I have allowed you to exert yourself too much in the past few days, darling."

"I don't know whether or not I have gone about too much, papa, but it was very kind of you to let me," she replied, laying her head on his shoulder, for they were sitting side by side on a sofa in the cabin, while the others had all gone up to the deck. "But, oh, I can't forget those poor men who perished in the flames yesterday or their wives and children—perhaps left very poor and helpless. Papa, if you are willing, I'd like to give all my pocket money to help them. My own dear father pays my way all the time, and I don't need to buy any of the fine things I see for sale here and there."

"My dear child," he said with emotion, "you may do just as you please about that. I am very glad that my little girl is so willing to deny herself to help others, and I must tell you for your comfort that a good deal of money has already been raised for the benefit of those sadly bereaved ones."

"You gave some, papa? Oh, I knew you would!"

"Yes, daughter, I gave out of the abundance of means which God has put into my hands—certainly not that it may all be spent upon myself and dearest ones, but it was entrusted to me that some of it may be used for the relief of suffering humanity. It is a very great pleasure—an inestimable privilege—to be permitted thus to allay to some extent the woes of poverty and bereavement."

"Yes, papa. I feel it so and am thankful that you approve of my doing what I can to help those poor, bereaved ones."

"I am very glad my little girl is unselfish enough to desire to do so," he responded. He passed a hand tenderly over her golden curls as he spoke and kissed her with the warmth of his affection.

"Do you want to join the others on the deck?" he asked presently. "Or would you rather go at once to your bed and rest? You are looking very weary."

"I am tired, papa," she replied. "But I think that to lie in one of the steamer chairs on deck and listen to the talk will rest me nicely."

"You may do so for an hour or two," he said. "I will help you up there, but when the others scatter—as they probably will by that time—I want you to go to your bed and try to get a good, long night's sleep. I must take good care of my feeble, delicate little girl that she may gain, and not lose, by this trip to the North and visit to the World's Fair."

He took her in his arms as he spoke, carried her to the deck, deposited her in a vacant lounging chair, and then seated himself by her side and took Neddie on his knee.

Violet was on her husband's other side, and Dr. Conly and his Marian near at hand on the farther side of Gracie.

"You are looking weary, little cousin," he remarked, giving her a searching look. "So weary that were I asked for a prescription it should be an early retirement to your berth, to be followed by a long night's rest. However, I suppose you are Harold's patient now."

"Yours, too, Cousin Arthur," she said with a smile. "Also papa's, and he has already given me the same prescription."

"As do I, if I am consulted," said Harold. "And when three such physicians agree, you surely will not venture to disregard their advice."

"No, indeed!" she returned with her own sweet smile again. "Nor would I, if any of the three had given it. I do really feel the need of rest for tonight, but I hope you will all agree to let me go at least as far as the Court of Honor tomorrow."

"That will depend upon how you are feeling in the morning," returned her father. Violet added, "And if you should have to stay here and rest for a day or two, you need not feel so badly about it, Gracie, because our time for remaining in and about the White City is not limited like that of some less fortunate people."

"No, mamma, that is something to be thankful for. Oh, I do think myself a most fortunate girl," Gracie said in reply, directing a look of ardent affection toward her father as she spoke. The other young folks were chatting together near by, principally of the beauties of the Fair, and indulging in many a merry jest and much light laughter.

"The Court of Honor is, in my opinion, the most beautiful place in the world," remarked Rosie. "At least, the most beautiful I have ever seen or can imagine—especially at night when the magnificent MacMonnie's fountain and the electric fountains are all at play. What beautiful, rainbow-colored showers they send up! I never dreamed of anything so lovely and can never weary of looking at them."

"Nor have I," said Croly. "I move that we all go over there presently in time to witness the lighting up of the fountains."

There was general assent, and young Percy Landreth, who had managed to secure a seat close at Lucilla's side, said to her in an undertone, "You will go surely, and may I have the pleasure of acting as your escort?"

"I don't know," she returned with a slight laugh and an arch look at Chester Dinsmore, who, sitting on her other side, had overheard the request, and was looking slightly vexed and disappointed. "Papa hasn't told me whether I may go tonight or not, and I'm 'a young thing who cannot leave her father' or go anywhere without his knowledge and consent. I'll ask him, however," she concluded, jumping up and hastening to the captain's side. "Papa," she asked, "can I go presently to the Court of Honor with the others and you, for I suppose you are going?"

"I think it likely that your mamma and I will be going after a little," he said in reply. "But Gracie is too weary to return there tonight, and you, too, would be better able to enjoy yourself at the Fair tomorrow should you go early to bed tonight. So, that is what I wish you to do."

"Indeed, papa, I am not very tired," she said half imploringly, half in vexation. "Mayn't I go?"

"You have my answer to that question, daughter," he replied in a tone so low that the words scarce reached any ear but hers. "I think it best for both you and Gracie that you should stay here with her, and surely you love your sister well enough to do so willingly—even if you had your father's consent to your going ashore for the evening?"

"Papa," said Gracie, overhearing the last of his sentences, "I would not have Lu miss the pleasant evening on shore on my account. I will go directly to bed and probably fall asleep at once."

"As I hope and believe Lucilla will as well," he returned with a glance of grieved displeasure bestowed upon his eldest daughter, which sent a remorseful pang to her heart.

"Oh, father, don't be vexed with me," she entreated low and tremulously, putting a hand into his as she spoke. "I am glad that I am under your orders. I am, indeed, and would not for anything leave dear Gracie alone."

"I am sure of it, daughter," he returned, pressing the hand affectionately as he spoke. "Also I think that tomorrow you will be thankful to me that you have had a rest from exertion and excitement."

"Yes, papa, I always find that your way is best, and I am very glad and thankful that I have such a kind, wise father."

"Well, Lu, did you get leave to go?" asked Rosie as Lucilla joined the circle of young people.

"No. Papa wishes me to stay here and get to bed early that I may be well rested for tomorrow's exertion in seeing the sights of the White City," Lucilla answered in a lively, cheerful tone that seemed to indicate entire satisfaction with her father's decision. She was in fact so remorseful over her momentary exhibition of willfulness that she felt as if she no longer cared for anything but to convince her dearly loved father of her penitence on account of it and her desire to do exactly as he directed.

"A wise and kind decision, Lu," remarked Herbert Travilla, overhearing what she said. "A rest now may save you from a serious breakdown some days or weeks hence."

"Yes, Uncle Herbert, I am well aware that such a father as mine is a very great blessing," she returned with a smile. "I only wish I were as good a daughter."

Just at that moment guns announced the setting of the sun, and the flags on the *Dolphin* and other vessels came down with the usual ceremonies. That over, those who intended to go ashore for the evening or the night began their preparations, which were such as to occupy but a few minutes. Violet put her little ones to bed, and the captain, who had carried a sleepy little Ned down to the stateroom, on coming out into the salon, found Lucilla there waiting to speak to him.

"Papa," she said humbly, "have you quite forgiven my crossness tonight when you refused to let me go ashore? I am very, very sorry for it, but I am perfectly satisfied now with your decision. I was the next minute, and, oh, I do love you dearly, dearly, though I can hardly expect you to believe it when—when I'm so ready to be rebellious," she added, hiding her face on his chest, for he had taken her into his arms the moment she began to speak.

"Yet I do believe it, my own darling," he replied in tender tones, smoothing her hair caressingly as he spoke. "I fully believe that you love me devotedly, though for a moment you indulged in the old rebellious spirit that used to cause so much pain to both you and me. However, this is almost the first time I have seen any show of it for two or three years. In all that time, you have been as willingly and cheerfully obedient as anyone could ask or expect a daughter to be."

"Oh, thank you, my dear father, for saying that!" she responded, lifting to his eyes beaming with happiness. "I do intend that it shall be my very last failure to be as promptly and cheerfully obedient as possible, for I know you never deny me anything unless you see that it is for my good, and I have never known you to make a mistake about that. Do you want Gracie and me to go to bed as soon as you and the others are gone?"

"I think it may be well for you to do so, but if you both prefer, you may stay on deck for another half hour."

"Then I will get ready for bed at once, papa, for I want to do exactly as you think best, and I know Gracie does also."

"Yes, I know she does. By the way, I must carry her down before I go. She is so weary, poor child," he said, hurrying up to the deck.

Lucilla waited only to see the others off, then joined her sister in their stateroom.

"You poor dear, you are so tired!" she exclaimed, noticing Gracie's weary expression and heavy eyes. "You must let me help you with your preparations for bed."

"Thank you, Lu," returned Gracie. "You are such a dear sister—always so kind and helpful to me, but I am sorry that for my sake you should lose the pleasure of going to the Court of Honor with the others tonight."

"Oh, Gracie, you know we always find out in the end that papa's way is the best for us both, and he refused my request for my own sake not only yours."

"Yes. He is the very kindest and best of fathers," said Gracie. "He never refuses any one of his children anything he can give them when he thinks it good for them."

"But now I must stop talking and go to sleep as quickly as possible, as he bade me when he brought me down here."

Both she and Lucilla were asleep in only a few minutes and awoke the next morning feeling greatly refreshed and rested.

❧ ❧ ❧ ❧ ❧

"Shall we visit the Turkish village today?" asked Violet at the breakfast table.

"I say aye to that," said Walter. "I want to see it and make some purchases there. I've heard that there is a street there with booths along on the side and a bazaar where one can buy various kinds of Turkish goods. I want to get some if only for curiosities."

"For a quarter you can go up in the restaurant and see the girls dance," said his sister Rosie, "or into the theater to look at a representation of Mohammedan home life and adventure. So Mr. Will Croly told me."

"Well, I don't know about going to the theater," returned Walter. "But I'd like to see their mosque with its minaret, at noon or sunset, when a real muezzin comes out and calls upon the faithful to remember Allah and give him glory."

"He does it at sunrise, too, doesn't he?" asked Evelyn Leland.

"Yes, but we'll never get over there in time for that. Some of our American folks don't know what he is about—not understanding his language—and imagine that he's selling popcorn or advertising the dancehouse, or maybe calling for somebody to come and help him down."

"How, Uncle Wal?" asked Neddie.

"With a ladder, I suppose."

"Do they bring it to him?"

"I don't think they have yet, Neddie. At least, I haven't heard of it. But wouldn't you like to go and see it all?"

"Yes, if papa will take me there, and mamma will go, too."

"How many would like to go?" asked the captain, and everyone responding in favor of so doing, the question was considered settled.

They set out at their usual early hour, met Harold and Herbert in the Peristyle, lingered a little in the Court of Honor, then made their way to the Turkish village, went through the booths and bazaar at the mosque, and heard the noon cry of the muezzin.

Then they visited an Arabian tent and the facsimile of a house in Damascus. In the tent, there were male and female Arabs sitting cross-legged—some of them boiling coffee, or making thin wafer cakes, while others played on odd-looking instruments and chanted in monotonous tones.

The party went into the house, found that it only contained one room—oblong in shape with a high ceiling and windows just beneath the cornice.

"That would hardly do for Americans," remarked Walter, gazing up at them. "For we could not see into the street."

"We could go to the door, Uncle Walter," said little Elsie.

"Or have a step ladder to carry about from one window to another," laughed Rosie.

"I like the festooned walls, the fountain in the center, and the thick rugs on the floors," remarked Violet. "The hanging lamps are lovely, the ornaments of rich woods inlaid with ivory, and the divans that look like such comfortable resting places."

"Yes, madam would find them pleasant to rest upon," responded a young Turk in excellent, but quaintly intoned, English. Then he went on to explain everything in the same tongue.

Their next visit was to Cairo Street, at the gate of which ten cents was asked for admission of each one of the party—a small sum they thought to give in payment for a sight of all that was on exhibition inside. Having passed through the gate, they found themselves in a street square with a café opening into it on one side. Entering it, they sat down and looked about them.

Captain Raymond, who had been more than once in Cairo itself, pronounced the scene an exact copy of what was to be found there, and they presently learned that the doors and the wooden-grated windows had been brought bodily from that city.

They could see projecting balconies, mysterious archways, airy loggias, and tiny shops filled to overflowing with such things as many a one would want to buy. Being in easy circumstances, they bought a number of articles such as were not too heavy or cumbersome to be easily carried.

Soon, however, their attention was turned to the crowds in the streets. Nearby was a donkey and camel stand—donkeys standing and camels lying down in their own peculiar fashion.

"Oh, what funny fellows!" laughed little Ned.

"Yes," said his father, "those are camels. Would you like to take a ride on one?"

"No, sir. I might fall off."

"Yes, Ned, and hurt yourself—maybe even break your leg. It would take even Cousin Arthur a good while to mend it, so that you would miss the pleasure of going about with the rest of us," said Walter.

"I don't want to ride just now," said Ned. "But if I did, I'd rather try one of those little horses."

"Donkeys, Ned," corrected his sister Lucilla. "What little fellows they are—no bigger that Max's dog, Prince!"

"Oh, I see one!" cried Rosie with a merry laugh. "That one going down the street knocked against that big, fat man and almost upset him."

"Notice the drivers," said Evelyn. "They are all so swarthy and with such black eyes, naked feet, long caftans, fez, and turbans. And what a keen watch they keep for customers. Evidently they do not despise American dollars, dimes, or cents."

"No, indeed! Not they," said Walter. "Oh, there are a couple who evidently contemplate taking a ride on a camel. See, the young fellow seems to be bargaining with one of the drivers, and how the people are crowding around to look and listen!"

"What's the price?" they heard the young man ask. They did not catch the reply, but he went on with his questions. "Will he bite? Is he quite tame? Is there any danger at all?"

"Not a bit," returned the driver. "A good camel," and as he spoke he reached for the girl, who shrank back a little. But he quickly lifted her to the saddle and showed her how to hold on.

Then the young man climbed up behind her, reached around her waist, and seized the handhold as if determined that nothing should tear it from his grasp.

The girl noticed and grew more frightened, turning a trifle paler and asking, "Is there any danger?"

But the driver was already tugging at the halter and striking the camel over the neck with his stick, and slowly it spread out its hind legs, rising on them first and throwing its riders forward till it seemed as if they must slide down his sloping neck and fall to the ground.

The girl screamed as her hat fell over her eyes, but both she and her escort held on with deathlike grip.

The camel paused for a moment and swayed back and forth sideways. The girl screamed again, but the camel was only untangling his legs. The next instant he had settled himself on them in a way that threw his riders backward so that they would have fallen off behind but for their firm grasp of the ropes.

By now the camel was fairly upon his four feet and was slowly turning round with a wobbling motion like a boat caught in a trough of waves. The riders had recovered from their fright, and they were both laughing. All this time, the crowd had been standing around watching the two, laughing and tittering, for, risky as the whole proceeding looked, there was really very little, if any, danger.

CHAPTER THIRTEENTH

"LET US GO NOW to the Guatemala Building," said Harold as they left Cairo Street. "I should like you all to see the grotto with its specimens of the fauna of the country, among which is a remarkable bird called the gavila. This remarkable bird sings upon the half hours with unvarying regularity, showing itself as correct as a sundial and almost as useful as a government observatory."

"Is it sure to wake and sing every half hour in the night, uncle?" asked little Elsie.

"Oh, no! It is only a day clock, Elsie. It stops attending to the business at sundown and begins again in the morning."

They were all interested in the strange bird, and the older people in a map, showing the location of the principal towns and railways, and in the exhibit that was located in an open court and about a fountain of the flora of the country. They also examined some pictures hung about the balcony, showing the principal places in the city of Guatemala and other large towns.

"I feel a particular interest in Korea at present," remarked Grandma Elsie as the left the Guatemala Building. "If entirely agreeable to the rest of you, I should like, now, to look at their exhibit in the Manufacturers' Building."

"Yes, mother. It is in the southwestern part," returned Harold, leading the way. "The booth is small, but it is crowded with exhibits. The Korean Royal Commissioner—with the name of Jeung Kiung Wow—has charge of it."

"That is a funny name, uncle," laughed Ned.

"And yet our names may have just as funny a sound to him," Violet said, smiling down at her little son.

When they reached the Korean booth, the first thing that attracted their attention was the flag hanging from it. The captain explained its design, the others listening with interest.

"It represents the male and female elements of nature," he said. "You see it is blue and yellow. The blue represents the heavenly, or male element, the yellow the earthly, or female. You see the heavens across the eastern sea, and they seem to lap over and embrace the earth, while the earth to landward rises in lofty mountains and folds the heavens in its embrace, so making a harmonious whole. The four characters around the central figure represent the four points of the compass."

They passed in and found a good many sights which interested them—banners and lanterns, a bronze table and dinner set for one person, a cupboard of dishes, a fire pot and tools, boots and shoes of leather, wood and straw, a kite and reel, a board on which is played a game resembling chess, white and blue vases, and a very old brass cannon used in the American attack on Korean forts in the seventies. Also there were banners hanging on the walls of the booth, and here and there stood screens, one of which was hand embroidered by the ladies of the palace.

On the dummies in the center of the room were shown ancient warriors' costumes, the court dress of both a military and a civil official, a lady's court dress, and various articles of footgear.

There was a map showing Korea and adjacent countries, and attached to it was a paper headed, "Questions Answered."

Mr. Dinsmore stood before it and read some of them aloud: "Korea and Corea are both correct, but the former is preferred. Korea is not part of China, but is independent. The Koreans do not speak the Chinese language, and their language resembles neither the Chinese nor the Japanese. Korea made treaties in 1882. All the articles are owned by the government. Korea has electric lights, steamships, telegraph, but no railroads. Koreans live in comfortable houses, heated by flues under the floor. Korean civilization is ancient and high; area one hundred thousand square miles; population sixteen million; climate like that of Chicago, country mountainous, mineral wealth undeveloped, agricultural products chiefly rice, beans, wheat, and corn."

"I am glad we came," remarked Rosie as they passed out of the booth. "I now know a good deal more about Korea than I did before and find it a far more interesting country than I had any idea that it was."

The next visit was to the rotunda of the Government Building, where they found many mural paintings of famous incidents in American history and scenes of the largest cities—so that it was a good representation of the whole country.

In the rotunda was a hollow section of one of the largest trees that grow in the Maraposa grove of redwoods in California. The interior was brilliantly lit by means of incandescent lights, and a platform at the top of the trunk was reached by an inside, winding stairway. The chamber walls were covered with photographs showing the grove from which the tree trunk was cut and how it was conveyed to the Fair and set up.

Beside the redwood, there were eight alcoves in the rotunda in which were many articles: colonial relics, such as the pipe which Miles Standish smoked, the first Bible brought to this country in 1620—the year of the landing of the Pilgrims, a piece of the torch Putnam used when he entered the wolf's cave, the fife of Benedict Arnold, and many others scarcely less interesting.

ꕥ ꕥ ꕥ ꕥ ꕥ

"I think my two eldest daughters have borne well the exertions of the day," the captain remarked with a smiling glance at them as they stood upon the deck of the *Dolphin*.

"Yes, father, thanks to your kind thoughtfulness in sending us so early to bed last night," returned Lucilla with a grateful, loving look up into his face. "The longer I live, the more thoroughly convinced I am that you always know what is best for me."

"That is just my experience, Lu," laughed Violet, standing near. "And I'll venture to assert that Gracie can say the same thing."

"Indeed, I can!" responded Gracie heartily. "It is a great satisfaction to have one so wise, kind, and good almost always at hand to decide doubtful questions for you."

"Tut! Tut! I do certainly wonder if there ever was any other man upon this earth who was so tried with so much gross flattery," exclaimed the captain in feigned displeasure.

At that moment, others stepped upon the deck, and their presence put an end to the bit of familiar family chat, Violet and her husband hastening to welcome their guests—for among the arrivals were Annis and several others from Pleasant Plains, whom they had not seen for some days. It was an easy matter for friends to miss each other among the crowds and the various buildings at the fair. Chester and Frank Dinsmore and Mr. Hugh Lilburn, who had not been seen there before, were also among the group.

"Why, how do you do, cousin? I did not know you had arrived in the city," said Violet, offering her hand.

"Very well, thank you. I arrived only last night," he said. "I was not able to hunt you up till now. Ah, father, Cousin Elsie, captain," shaking hands with each in turn. "It does one good to see all your kind, pleasant faces."

"And us to see yours," returned Violet. "But where are Ella and your boy?"

"At home," he answered. "At least that's where I left them."

"But why didn't you bring them along?" asked his father. "The bit laddie is not likely to have another chance to look at such sights as one may see here today."

"His mother thought him rather young for that, seeing he is not very far along in his second year," replied Hugh. "Nor could she be persuaded to leave him behind. He is a person of great consequence in his mother's eyes, is my little Ronald, if in no other."

"Ah, I can understand that," laughed Violet. "But now, Cousin Hugh, you must let me have the pleasure of introducing you to our cousins from Pleasant Plains."

It was quite a gathering of relatives and friends, all weary enough with the day's exertions in sightseeing to enjoy resting in comfortable chairs on the vessel's deck while comparing notes as to their experiences since coming to the Fair. They discussed what each had seen and heard and what they were planning yet to see, some caring more especially for one class of curiosities, some for another.

Hardly a half-hour had passed when they were summoned to an excellent repast, after which they again repaired to the deck, where they gathered in groups and indulged in further chat.

Gracie was a little apart from the others, reclining in a steamer chair.

"Are you very, very tired, Gracie?" asked Walter, coming to her side.

"Pretty tired," she answered, smiling up into his face. "Why? Did you want me to do anything?"

"Oh, no. No, indeed! But I was just thinking that now that we have two ventriloquists here, we might have some fun—for so far as I know, the folks from Pleasant Plains don't know anything about the extraordinary powers of Cousins Ronald and Hugh. I hoped you weren't too tired to enjoy it."

"I don't believe I am," she laughed. "I think I shall enjoy it if papa doesn't send me to bed too soon. It was good of you to think of me, Walter."

"Was it, when you are the girl who always thinks of everybody else?"

"Not always, Walter. I am afraid I very often think of myself first."

"Do you? I never knew it before," he laughed. Hurrying to old Mr. Lilburn's side, he whispered something in his ear.

The old gentleman smiled and gave a nod of assent. "I like to please you, laddie," he said in an undertone. "So does Hugh, and mayhap atween us, we can accomplish something worthwhile."

"Oh, thank you," returned Walter. "I do think, cousin, that a little fun would do us all good. We've been dining heartily—at least I have—and I think a good laugh assists digestion."

Hugh sat near, chatting with Captain Raymond. Walter now turned to him with a whispered request that he seemed to grant as readily as his father had the one made of him.

At that Rosie and Lucilla, who were watching Walter with apparent interest in his proceedings, exchanged a glance of mingled amusement and satisfaction, while Gracie, whose eyes were following his movements, laughed softly to herself. She, too, was in the mood for a bit of fun, and she saw in all this the promise of some.

"Dear me, what a lot o' folks! And all lookin' so comfortable like. They've had a good dinner—or supper, whichever they call it—you bet, Joe, while we're as hungry as bears," said a rough, masculine voice that seemed to come from a spot close to Captain Raymond's rear.

Before the sentence was half finished, every other voice was hushed, and all eyes were turned in the direction from which the sound seemed to come. Everyone was quite startled for an instant, but by the time the sentence was finished, the captain looked perfectly calm and cool.

"Who are you? And how did you come aboard the vessel, sir?" he asked.

"In the boat, sir, same as the rest o'e company," was the reply in the same voice.

"Without waiting for an invitation, eh?"

"Humph! Might 'a' missed it if we'd waited. Say, captain, are you mean enough to let us fellows go hungry when you have a vessel full o' good things for eatin'? To say nothing of a pocket full o' tin?"

"'If any would not work, neither should he eat,'" quoted the captain. "What work have you two been about today?"

"Same as yerself, sir. We been lookin' at the exhibits in this here big World's Fair."

"Very well. You may go and ask the steward for some supper."

A sound of retreating footsteps followed, and those of the guests who were not in on the secret looked about here and there in blank astonishment.

"Well, really! Am I going blind?" exclaimed young Percy Landreth, passing his hand over his eyes in a bewildered way. "I couldn't see either of those fellows at all."

"Oh, no!" said Lucilla. "One can sometimes hear what one cannot see."

But at that instant there was a "cluck, cluck," as of a hen which seemed to come from Annis's lap, at which she sprang to her feet with a slight cry of astonishment and dismay. Seeing nothing, "Why, where is it?" she asked half breathlessly, and the "cluck, cluck," was repeated apparently from behind the chair of her next neighbor, which was immediately followed by a loud barking as if a dog were in chase of the chicken.

"Oh!" exclaimed Annis, turning her eyes upon the elder Mr. Lilburn. "I think I know. I've think I've heard—"

But a warning gesture from Violet, whose face was full of amusement, stopped her, and she dropped into her chair again with a slight, mirthful laugh and a look of relief and diversion.

Percy saw it and suddenly comprehended pretty accurately what was going on. Yet, at the same moment, he was startled and annoyed by a loud buzzing about his ears as though a bee were flying round and round his head. He put up his hand and tried to knock it away. Then it seemed to fly to Chester, and though he was wholly acquainted with the powers of Cousin Ronald and Hugh, he, too, made an effort to dodge and drive it away.

Then the squeak of a mouse came from a reticule on Lucilla's lap so unexpectedly that she gave a little scream, at the same time springing to her feet and throwing the reticule from her.

At that, her father laughed. She picked it up again and reseated herself with a slightly mortified air.

"Let me get that mouse for you, Lu," said Herbert, holding out his hand for the reticule, but scarcely were the words out of his mouth, when the meow of a kitten, coming from his coat pocket, caused him to involuntarily clap his hand upon it.

"Yes, Uncle Herbert, take the mouse out and give it to the cat," returned Lulu quickly, handing the reticule to him as she spoke.

"Thank you," he returned laughingly. "I really don't believe the creature is hungry."

"Oh, uncle, let me see that kitty!" cried Ned, running to him.

"Put your hand into my pocket and try to find it," was the good-humored reply, and Neddie at once availed himself of the permission.

"Why, it isn't there!" he exclaimed. "How do you s'pose it got out?"

"I'm inclined to think it never got in, Ned," said his uncle.

"Oh, it's in mine!" cried the little fellow excitedly, clapping his hand upon his pocket as a pitiful meow seemed to come from it. "Why, I can't feel it. Papa," running to him, "please, take it out, I can't find it."

The captain took hold of the pocket. "You made a mistake, son. It isn't there. I feel nothing but your handkerchief and a few other soft articles."

"Why—why, how strange!" exclaimed the little fellow. "I was sure I heard it in there, papa. Oh, what is that?" as the squeal of a young pig seemed to come from his father's pocket. At the same instant, the loud and furious bark of a big dog seemed to come from some place in his rear very near at hand. With a little cry of affright, he made haste to climb upon his father's knee for protection, putting his arms about his neck and clinging tightly to him.

But just then a loud cry came from below. "Help! Help! These rascally fellows are stealing the silver! Captain Raymond, sir, help, or they'll throttle me!"

At that, the captain sprang to his feet, set Ned in his mother's lap, and hurried below, while the young men rose hastily to go to his assistance, even those of them who were well acquainted with Cousin Ronald's powers, thinking for an instant that the alarm was real. But a laugh of amusement from him and his son let them into the secret that it was but a false alarm, the trick of a ventriloquist, and they resumed their seats as hastily as they had arisen from them.

"Oh, oh!" cried Ned. "I'm so afraid my dear papa will get hurt! Uncle Harold and Uncle Herbert, won't you go and help papa fight those bad men? Please, go quick! Oh, please do!"

"Oh, no, Neddie, papa is so big and strong that he doesn't need any help to make such fellows behave themselves," said Lucilla. "And here he comes all safe and sound," as the captain stepped upon the deck again.

"Well, captain," said Grandma Elsie, looking up smilingly into his face as he drew near, "did you catch the rogues?"

"No, mother, I could not find the least trace of them," he answered gravely. Then turning to the elder Mr. Lilburn, "Cousin Ronald," he asked, "do you think you would know them if you were to see them, sir?"

"Me know them, captain?" exclaimed the old gentleman in well-feigned astonishment. "Can it be possible you mean to insinuate that I am the kind who would associate with beggars and thieves?"

"I mean no offense, sir," returned the captain with a twinkle of fun in his eye. "But it sometimes happens that a very honest and honorable man may be well acquainted with the appearance of some dastardly villain."

"I'm no sich a character as that," snarled a rough voice that seemingly came from a part of the deck in Mr. Lilburn's rear and sounded very much like the one which had demanded some supper a short time before. "An' I hope it isn't me you're ameanin', fer I'm as honest an' decent a man as any in this crowd, ef I do say it, that shouldn't."

"Who is that man? I couldn't see him the other time, and I can't see him now," exclaimed little Elsie, gazing round in wide-eyed wonder. She had never quite understood Cousin Ronald's performances, and she was much puzzled to comprehend all that was now being done and said.

"I say, capting," cried another strange voice, it also apparently coming from an invisible speaker, "why upon airth don't you put that impident critter off the boat? I'd do it in a jiffy if 'twas me."

"You have my permission to do so, sir," returned the captain. "But perhaps he will go presently of his own accord."

"Hollo!" shouted a strange voice that seemed to come from the water near at hand and was followed immediately by the dip of an oar, "I say, what's the matter up there on that deck? If I was capting o' that yacht, there shouldn't be no such goings on aboard it."

"The impudence of the fellow!" exclaimed Lucilla, forgetting for the moment the presence of two ventriloquists. Springing up, she was about to rush for the side of the vessel to get a sight of the boatman.

Her father, turning toward her with a smile, laid a detaining hand on her arm, while at the same time he called out in good-humored tones, "Suppose you board us then, sir, and show what you can do."

"Humph!" snarled the voice that seemed so near at hand. "You'd better try it, old feller, whomsoever you be, but I bet you'll find me an' Joe here more'n a match fer you."

"Oh, Bill, I say, let's git out o' this!" exclaimed a third voice, apparently close at hand. "We've had our fill o' grub and might as well make ourselves scarce now."

"All right, Joe," returned the voice of the first speaker. "We'll git inter that feller's boat, and no doubt he'll take us ashore to git rid of us."

A sound as of retreating footsteps followed, then all was quiet.

"Very well done, Cousin Ronald. One could almost see those fellows," laughed the captain.

"I couldn't see them, papa," said little Elsie. "I could only hear them. What was the reason?"

"Suppose you ask Cousin Ronald," was her father's reply.

"So you are a ventriloquist, sir?" remarked Percy Landreth in a tone between assertion and inquiry, giving the old gentleman a look of mingled curiosity and amusement.

"You think so, do you, sir? But why should I be suspected more than anyone else in this company of friends and relatives?" asked Cousin Ronald in a quiet tone.

"Well, sir, it seems to me evident from all I have seen and heard. All here appear to look to you as one who is probably at the bottom of all these mysterious doings."

"No, not quite all, Percy," Violet said with a slight smile.

"So there are two, are there?" queried Percy. "Then the other, I presume, is Mr. Hugh Lilburn."

"Oh, Percy!" cried Lucilla in half reproachful tones. "I wish you hadn't found out quite so soon. It spoils the fun!"

"Oh, no, not quite, I think," he returned. "For I noticed that even those who must have been in on the secret were occasionally taken by surprise."

"Yes," she admitted with a laugh. "I did think for a moment that there was a man calling to us from a boat down there on the lake and that there was a mouse in my reticule."

Chapter Fourteenth

SIGHTSEEING WAS resumed again the next day, much time being spent in the Manufacturers' and Liberal Arts' Buildings. It was the marvel of the Exposition, covering more than forty acres of ground, and filled with curious and beautiful things from almost every quarter of the globe. Hours were spent there, and then a ride in an electric boat on the lagoon was taken as a restful form of recreation.

The greater part of the afternoon was spent in the ever-fascinating Midway Plaisance, and then the group returned to the yacht for their evening meal and an hour or two of restful chat in the easy chairs on its deck. With the setting of the sun, the older ones returned to the Court of Honor, leaving the children in bed and under the ever-watchful care of their nurses.

Much the same sort of life continued for a week or more, but then many of the friends found it necessary to return to their homes. The cousins from Pleasant Plains were among that number, and the day before leaving, young Percy seized a rare opportunity for a word of private chat with Captain Raymond.

"I have been coveting such a chance as this, sir," he said, coloring with embarrassment. "But—but couldn't find it till now. I—I—want—"

"Speak out, my young friend," said the captain kindly. "I am ready to listen to whatever you may have to say, and if in my power to assist you in any way, I shall feel it a pleasure to do so—particularly as you are a relative of my wife."

Percy had had but little opportunity for showing his penchant for Lucilla, and the young girl's father was not thinking of her. He imagined there might be some business venture in which the young man desired his assistance.

"You have perhaps something to tell me of your plans and prospects for the future," he said inquiringly. "And if so, possibly I may be able to exert influence, or render assistance, in some way. It would give me pleasure, I assure you, to do anything in my power. So, do not be afraid to speak out."

"You are very kind, captain, very kind indeed," stammered Percy, flushing more hotly than before. "But that—that is not it exactly. I hope you won't be angry, but I have been trying to get up my courage to ask for—something far more valuable than money, influence, or anything else that could be thought of. I—I love your daughter, sir, Miss Lucilla—and—and I hope you won't forbid me to tell her so."

Percy drew a sigh of relief that at last the Rubicon was crossed, and his desire and purpose made known. But a glance at the captain's both grave and troubled face dashed his hopes to the ground.

A moment of silence followed, and then Captain Raymond spoke in gentle, sympathetic tones.

"I am sorry, very sorry to disappoint you, my young friend, but I cannot grant your request. Lucilla is but a child yet—a mere schoolgirl. And such I intend to keep her for some six years or more to come. I have no objection to you more than any other man, but I cannot consent to allowing her to be approached on that subject until she reaches more mature years."

"And in the meantime, somebody will in all probability get ahead of me," sighed Percy. "Oh, sir, can I not persuade you to revoke that decision and let me at least learn from her own lips whether or not she cares for me?"

"I think I can furnish all the information you wish in that line," returned the captain, laying a kindly hand on the young man's shoulder. "For hardly an hour ago she told me—as she has many times before—that she loved no one else in the wide world half so dearly as her father."

"Well, sir, I am glad of it, since you won't let me speak yet," said Percy with a rueful sort of smile. "But—please, don't blame me for it—but I can't feel satisfied to be forbidden to speak a word, considering how very far apart our homes are and that we may not meet again for years, if ever. I also must consider Chester Dinsmore, who is, I can see plainly enough, over head and ears in love with her and will be near her all the time and have every chance to cut me out."

"No," said the captain. "I shall give him no chance, either. I fully intend keeping my little girl to myself—as I have already told you—for at least six or eight years to come."

"You have no objection to me personally, sir?"

"None whatever. In fact, from all I have seen and heard, I am inclined to think you a fine fellow—almost equal to my own boy, Max," Captain Raymond said with a smile. "If my daughter were of the right age and quite ready and willing to leave her father, I should have but one objection to your suit—that you would take her so far away from me."

"Possibly I might not, sir, should there be an opening for me near where you reside. I believe the Bible says it is the man who is to leave father and mother and cleave to his wife."

"True, my young friend," returned the captain. "But the time I have set is too far away to make it worth our while to consider that question at present."

With that the interview closed, the two parted. However, the captain was to be confronted only a few minutes later by Chester Dinsmore with a like request to that just denied to Percy.

"No, no, Chester," he said. "It is not to be thought of. Lucilla is entirely too young to leave her father's fostering care and take up the duties and trials of married life. I cannot consent to your saying a word to her on the subject for years to come."

"You have no objection to me personally, I trust, sir?" returned the young man, looking chagrined and mortified.

"None whatever," Captain Raymond hastened to say. "I have just given the same answer to another suitor, and there is one consideration that inclines me to prefer you to him—namely, that you are a near neighbor to us at Woodburn. So, if I were ever to give up my daughter to you, I should feel the parting much less than if she were about to make her home so far north as this."

"Well, sir, that's a crumb of comfort. Though, to be often in her company, seeing her lovely face and watching her pretty ways will make it all the more difficult to refrain from showing my esteem, admiration, and love. In fact, I don't know how to stand it. Excuse me, captain, but what harm could there be in telling her my story and trying to win my way to her heart—provided, of course, that I spoke of marriage only as something to be looked for in the far off future?"

"No, I cannot consent to that, Chester," returned the captain with decision. "It would only put mischief in her head and rob her of childlike simplicity. She is still too young to know her own mind on that subject and might fancy that she had given her heart to one who would, a few years later, be entirely distasteful to her. But I trust you, Chester, not to breathe a word to her of your—what shall I call it—admiration, until you have my consent."

"It is more than admiration, sir!" exclaimed Chester. "I love her as I never loved anything before in my life, and it would just about kill me to see her in the possession of another."

"Then comfort yourself that for years to come no one's suit will be listened to any more favorably than yours," returned the father of the girl he so coveted. And with that, the interview came to an hasty end.

Their conversation had been held at one end of the deck while the rest of the party sat chatting together at the other. The Captain and Chester joined them now and entered into the talk, which ran principally upon the fact that all the relatives from Pleasant Plains must leave for home the very next day.

"How would you all like to go by water?" asked Captain Raymond, as if the thought of such a possibility had just struck him.

"I do not believe the idea has occurred to any of us," replied Annis. "Since the building of the railroad, so few make the journey by water that the boats running on our river are few, small, and I presume not remarkably comfortable."

"How would this one answer?" he asked. "It is but thirty-eight miles across the lake. I think we would find your river navigable nearly or quite up to your town. To reach it from here would not take more than six or eight hours."

"Then they could all go, as they need not all spend the night, or any part of it, on board," exclaimed Violet in tones of delight. "Oh, Cousin Annis and all of you, do agree to it, and we will have a charming little trip!"

"Indeed, so far as I am concerned nothing could be more pleasant, I am sure," said Annis, looking highly pleased. "But—I fear it would be giving you a great deal of trouble, captain."

"Not at all," he returned. "On the contrary, it will, I think, be a very enjoyable little trip to me and my wife and children."

"Oh, I should like it very much!" exclaimed Lucilla. "There would be such a nice, large party of us all the way to Pleasant Plains, supposing your river is navigable so far for a vessel of this size. And the trip up the lake, a little visit to Mackinaw, and the sail back again, would be a restful and enjoyable break in the visit here to the Fair."

"What do you say to the plan, Grandpa and Grandma Dinsmore, mother?" asked the captain, turning toward them. "And you, Cousin Ronald?"

All expressed themselves as well pleased with the idea, and it was decided to carry it out.

"We will be happy to have you accompany us also, Chester and Frank, should you care to do so," said the captain cordially. "Though I fear it will rob you of some of the time you had planned to spend at the Fair."

"Thank you, captain," said Frank. "I, for one, accept your very kind invitation with great pleasure. It will give me a glimpse of a part of our big country that I have never seen, and we shall be in the most pleasant of company, too. As to our visit to the Fair, we can prolong it by another week, if we choose to do so."

"So we can," said his brother. "And I, too, accept your kind invitation, captain, with cordial thanks."

"Then let me advise you of Pleasant Plains to be on board here, bag and baggage, by eight, or at the latest nine, o'clock tomorrow morning," said Captain Raymond. "We will be happy to have you take breakfast here with us, and we may as well be on our way across the lake while eating. Then, I hope to have you at your destination by seven or eight in the evening. Leaving you there, we can steam on down the river and up the lake, the rest of my passengers resting in their berths as usual."

"Then it will take about all of the next day to get to Mackinaw. Won't it, papa?" asked Gracie.

"Probably."

"And how long will we stay there?"

"I suppose that will depend upon how we enjoy ourselves. I think it likely you will all be satisfied with a day or two, as there is so much that will interest you here which you have not seen."

"Cousin Annis," said Violet, "would you not be willing to make one of our party? I am sure that with a little crowding, we could accommodate you very easily."

"Thank you very much, cousin," replied Annis. "But I fear my company would not repay you for the necessary crowding."

At that, several voices exclaimed that it certainly would. The younger girls added that they could crowd a little closer together without feeling it any inconvenience, and the captain said laughingly that impromptu beds would have to be provided in the salon for Chester and Frank. He went on to say that he would join them there, so leaving a vacant place for her with his wife. With a little more persuasion, Annis accepted the invitation, knowing that she could be well spared for a time from the large circle of brothers and sisters, nephews and nieces, as her dear old father and mother had been taken some years before to their heavenly home.

"I wish we could take Cousin Arthur, Marian, and Hugh with us," said Violet. "They are not here tonight, but they must still be in the city, I think."

"Yes," said her husband. "And I think we might manage to accommodate them also, should they care to go, but probably they will prefer having that much more time to spend at the Fair."

It was a beautiful moonlight evening, and after a little more chat in regard to the arrangements to be made for the morrow's journey, all except the children, who were already in bed, went together to the Court of Honor. They wandered down the Midway Plaisance, then to the Ferris Wheel, in which everyone was desirous to take a ride by moonlight. None there were by any means disappointed in the ride.

On leaving the Ferris Wheel, they bade each other goodnight and scattered to their several resting-places—the cousins to their boarding house, the others to the yacht.

A little before eight o'clock the next morning, there was a cheerful bustle on board the *Dolphin*. The extra passengers arrived safely and in good season with their luggage and found everything on the boat in good trim. An excellent breakfast awaited them and the others of the party.

The weather was all that could be desired. They were in congenial spirits, and the day passed most delightfully. But though the young people were very sociable, no one seeming to be under any restraint, neither Chester nor Percy found an opportunity for any private chat with Lucilla. The fact was that the captain had had a bit of a private talk with his wife and her mother, in which he gave them an inkling into the state of affairs as concerned the two young men and his eldest daughter. He requested their assistance in preventing either one from so far monopolizing the young girl's time as to be tempted into letting her into the secret of his feelings toward her.

They reached Pleasant Plains early in the evening, landed the cousins belonging there with the single exception of Miss Annis Keith, then turned immediately and went down the river again, reaching the lake about the usual time for retiring to their berths.

The rest of their voyage was as delightful as that of the first day had been and was spent in a similar manner. As they sat together on the deck, toward evening, Gracie asked her father if Mackinaw had not been the scene of something interesting in history.

"There was a dreadful massacre there many years ago," he replied. "It occurred in 1763, by the Indians under Pontiac, an Indian chief. It was at the time of his attack on Detroit. There is a cave shown on the island in which the whites took refuge, but the Indians kindled a fire at its mouth and smoked them—men, women, and children—to death."

"Oh, how dreadful, papa! How very dreadful!" she exclaimed.

"Yes," he said, "those were frightful times, but often the poor Indians were really less to blame than the whites, who urged them on. The French urged them against the English, and the English urged them on against the Americans.

"Pontiac was the son of an Ojibway woman and chief of that tribe and of the Ottawas and Pottawattamies, who were in alliance with the Ojibways. In 1746, he and his warriors defended the French at Detroit against an attack by some of the northern tribes, and in 1755, he took part in their fight with Braddock, acting as the leader of the Ottawas."

"I wonder," said Gracie, as her father paused for a moment in his narrative, "if he was the Indian who, in that fight, aimed so many times at Washington, yet failed to hit him. Finally, he at last gave up the attempt to kill him, concluding that he must be under the special protection of the Great Spirit."

"That I cannot tell," her father said. "Whoever that Indian may have been, I think he was right in his conclusion—that God protected and preserved our Washington that he might play the important part he did in securing his country's freedom.

"But to return to my story. Pontiac hated the English. Though after the surrender of Quebec, some years after Braddock's defeat, finding that the French had been driven from Canada, he acquiesced in the surrender of Detroit to the English. He persuaded four hundred Detroit Indians, who were lying in ambush, intending to cut off the English there, to relinquish their design.

"But he hated the English, and in 1762, he sent messengers to every tribe between the Ottawa and the Mississippi to engage them all in a war of extermination against the English."

"Americans, too, papa?" asked little Elsie, who, sitting upon his knee, was listening very attentively to his narrative.

"Yes," he replied. "Our States were English colonies then, for the War of the Revolution did not begin until about thirteen years later. The messengers of Pontiac carried with them the red-stained tomahawk and a wampum war belt, the Indian fashion of indicating that war was purposed. Those to whom the articles were sent were thus invited to take part in the conflict.

"All the tribes to whom they were sent joined in the conspiracy, and the end of May was decided upon as the time when their bloody purpose should be carried out, each tribe disposing of the garrison of the nearest fort. Then all were to act together in an attack upon the settlements.

"On April 27, 1763, a great council was held near Detroit, at which Pontiac made an oration detailing the wrongs and indignities the Indians had suffered at the hands of the English and prophesying their complete extermination.

"He told also of a tradition that a Delaware Indian had been admitted into the presence of the Great Spirit, who told him that his race must return to the customs and weapons of their ancestors, throw away those they had gotten from the white men, abjure whiskey, and take up the hatchet against the English. 'These dogs dressed in red,' he called them, 'who have come to rob you of your hunting grounds and drive away the game.'

"Pontiac's own particular task was the taking of Detroit. The attack was to be made on the seventh of May. But the commander of the fort was warned of their intentions by an Indian girl, and in consequence when Pontiac and his warriors arrived on the scene, they found the garrison prepared to receive them. Yet, on the twelfth he surrounded the fort with his Indians. He was not able to keep a close siege, however, and the garrison was provided food by the Canadian settlers."

"These same settlers supplied the Indians also, did they not, my dear?" asked Violet.

"Yes," replied the captain. "They received in return, promissory notes drawn on birch bark and signed with the figure of an otter. It is said that all of them were afterward redeemed by Pontiac, who had issued them."

"That speaks well for the honesty of the Indians even if they were savage and cruel," remarked Walter. "In fact, they were hardly more cruel than some of the whites have been to them and to other whites with whom they were at war."

"Quite true," said the captain.

"But didn't the rest of the English try to help those folks in that fort at Detroit, papa?" asked little Elsie.

"Yes. Supplies and reinforcements were sent in schooners by way of Lake Erie, but they were captured by the Indians, who then compelled their prisoners to row them to Detroit, concealed in the bottom of the boat, hoping in that way to take the fort by stratagem. But, fortunately for the besieged, they were discovered before they could land.

"Afterward, another schooner filled with supplies and ammunition succeeded in reaching the fort, though the Indians repeatedly tried to destroy it by fire-rafts.

"Now the English thought themselves strong enough to attack the Indians, and on the night of July 31, 1763, 250 men set out for that purpose.

"But the Canadians had learned their intention and told the Indians. So, Pontiac was ready and waiting to make an attack, which he did as soon as the English were far enough from their fort for him to do so with advantage, firing upon them from all sides and killing and wounding fifty-nine of them. That fight is known as the fight of Bloody Bridge.

"On the twelfth of October the siege was raised, and the chiefs of the hostile tribes with the exception of Pontiac sued for pardon and peace. Pontiac was not conquered and retired to the country of the Illinois. In 1769, he was murdered in Cahokia—a village on the Mississippi near St. Louis. The deed was done by an Indian, who had been bribed to do it by an English trader."

"Papa, you have not told us yet what happened at Mackinac," said Lucilla.

"It, along with many other forts, was taken by Pontiac's Indians. All the inhabitants of the island were massacred," replied the captain. "There is a cave shown in a hillside some little distance out from the village in which the French sought refuge. They were there smoked to death, the Indians kindling fires at its mouth."

"Oh," exclaimed Gracie, "I am glad I didn't live in those dreadful days!"

"Yes," said her father. "We have great reason for gratitude that the lines have fallen to us in such pleasant places and times of peace."

Chapter Fifteenth

THE *DOLPHIN* LAY at anchor in Mackinac Bay only a day or two, in which time her passengers visited the fort, the village, and the cave of which Captain Raymond had spoken as the scene of that dreadful slaughter of the French by the Indians. Then the party started upon their return voyage to Chicago.

They were still favored with pleasant weather and passed most of the time on deck. Mr. Lilburn seemed to appreciate the society of Miss Annis Keith, generally contriving to get a seat in her immediate vicinity and to engage her in conversation. That did not strike anyone as strange, however, for Annis was a general favorite with both old and young, she showing a cousinly regard for all her relatives, especially for Mrs. Travilla, as the two had been almost lifelong friends. In these few days that they had been together they had had many private chats in which they recalled their early experiences at Pleasant Plains and the Oaks, and Elsie had urged Annis to return with her to Ion and spend the coming winter there.

This invitation Annis was considering, and the more she thought upon it the stronger grew her own inclination to accept it. But she must go home first to make some arrangements and preparations, she said.

The two were conversing together thus, as they drew near the end of their little trip, not caring that their talk might be audible to those about them.

"Surely it is not necessary that you should take much time for preparation, Annis," remarked Mr. Dinsmore. "We of Ion and its vicinity have an abundance of stores and dressmakers near at hand. And you had better see all that you can of the Fair now, for it will soon be a thing of the past."

"That is true, Cousin Annis," said the captain. "You'd better stay with us and see as much as possible."

"You are all very kind, cousins," she answered. "But I fear I am crowding you."

"Not at all," he and Violet replied, speaking together. Violet added, "We have all slept quite comfortably, and in the daytime there is certainly an abundance of room."

"If you do not stay, Cousin Annis," Rosie said with a merry look, "we will all have to conclude that you have not had room enough to make you quite comfortable."

"Then I certainly must stay," returned Annis with a smile, "if my going would give so entirely false an impression. Since I have had abundance of room and a most delightful time."

"Then you will stay on?"

"Yes, for a while, but I must go home for a day or two at least before leaving for the South."

"We will let you know our plans in season for that," the captain promised, and the matter was considered settled.

When her passengers awoke the next morning, the *Dolphin* was lying at her old anchorage near the beautiful Peristyle.

All had returned rested and refreshed and were eager to go on shore in search of further entertainment and instruction.

The greater part of the day was spent in the Midway Plaisance. They visited the Lapland family of King Bull, the most prominent character in that village, and found them all seated beside their odd-looking hut, which, like the others in that village, was made of skin, tent-like in shape, and banked with moss. The entrance was very small, and the door made of a piece of wood. A fire was kept burning in the center of the house in the ground. There was no chimney; some of the smoke escaped through a little hole in the roof if the wind was right. But if the wind came from the wrong direction the smoke stayed in the house, and the people enjoyed it. It did not, however, improve their complexions, which are said to be in their native state, not unlike the color of a well-cured ham.

King Bull they found had the largest house, and a very large family.

The Laplanders marry young, and it is not unusual for a grandfather to be under twenty-five years of age. King Bull was 112 years old and had great-great-great-great-great-grandchildren, and every day he played for a little while with the youngest of those.

These friends learned that King Bull had with him a son, Bals Bull, who was ninety years old. Bals had a son aged seventy-three, and he had a daughter aged fifty-nine. She had a son aged forty-one, who had a son aged twenty-nine, who had a daughter aged fourteen, and she had a daughter two years old.

"Dear me!" exclaimed Rosie on hearing this. "How old it makes a body feel! Why, just think! The mother of that two-year-old child is a year younger than you, Gracie Raymond, and you don't consider yourself much more than a child yet, do you?"

"No, indeed! And I don't want to be anything but my father's own little girl," returned Gracie, giving him a loving look that said more than her words.

"Can you tell us if this looks like the real Lapland village, Harold?" asked Walter.

"I am told it does," replied his brother. "I suppose it is nearly as possible a reproduction of one, though of course, it is not very large, there being but twenty-four Laplanders here."

"What do they eat, papa?" asked little Elsie.

"Fish, reindeer meat, and cheese made of the milk. The reindeer is their most valuable possession. Its skin is used for clothing; the fur is woven into cloth; they drink the milk and use the bones in the making of their sledges. They live entirely on such food during their winters, which are nine months long."

"And their summer only three months," said Evelyn. "I shouldn't like that."

"No, nor should I," said Herbert. "I think it must be by far the most enjoyable part of the year for me, for it is usually spent at the seashore."

"Are they heathen folks, papa?" asked Elsie.

"Most of them are Lutherans," he answered. "Now let us go to the reindeer park." They did so, found nine of the gentle creatures there, and saw them get a bath of Lake Michigan water from a hose-pipe, which they were told was given them three times daily. Then they were harnessed to their sledges and driven around the park, as they are driven in their own country. After that, they ran races, and then they were fed and milked.

The children had been deeply interested in the gentle reindeer and seemed loath to leave them when the performance was over. They were most delighted were three baby ones—two born on the way over to this country and one shortly after they reached Chicago, which was named Columbia.

"Now where shall we go next?" asked Rosie.

"Suppose we try the diving exhibit," said Walter. "It is something I should like to see." They found it on the south side of Midway Plaisance in a small building surrounding a huge tank of water. On the balcony of its second story stood a man turning a force pump, which seemed to attract a good deal of attention from the passersby.

Each visitor paid ten cents at the door and passed up a rude stairway by which he reached the surface of the water. There, a lecturer was seated who explained how the air was made to enter the diver's armor and how it left it. Then people were invited to throw small coins into the water. Captain Raymond put a bright dime into the hand of each of his younger children, and they gleefully tossed them in. The diver was in the bubbling water. They could not see him, but presently, through a telephone, he gave the dates on the coins. Then he came up to the surface of the water carrying a dummy that looked like a drowned man and let the visitors see him in is armor.

"He looks just like that picture of him that we saw outside," remarked little Elsie. "Ugh! I don't think I should ever be willing to wear such clothes."

"Armor." corrected her mother in a mirthful tone. "No, dear, I should not want to see you dressed in that style, unless to save you from drowning."

Just then, Mr. Dinsmore rose and led the way down another rough staircase, the others following.

Reaching the lower story, they found a great many peepholes through which they could look in upon the water of the tank. To each of these holes the diver came in turn, holding up a card on which was printed a farewell compliment. His hands looked shriveled and soaked, and Gracie and the other young girls afterward expressed sincere pity for him, saying they thought his life must be a hard one.

On leaving the diving exhibit, they went to the Fisheries Building, which they found very beautiful. In its east pavilion was a double row of grottoed and illuminated aquaria containing the strangest inhabitants of the deep. Here they saw bluefish, sharks, catfish, billfish, goldfish, rays, trout, eels, sturgeon, anemones, king crabs, burr fish, flounders, toad fish, and many other beautiful or remarkable inhabitants of the great deep. The illuminated and decorated aquaria showed them to great advantage. It was said that nothing so beautiful had hitherto been seen west of London.

The surface of the water in the aquaria was many feet above the heads of even the gentlemen of the party, but there were nearly six hundred feet of glass front, so that everybody could have a good view of the strange and beautiful creatures within. They all watched them for some time with curiosity and interest, the little folks questioning their papa about one and another variety, which were definitely new to them, but old acquaintances to one who had spent so many years upon the sea.

"Papa," said Elsie, "there is one that looks a good deal like a flower. Is it a live thing? What is its name, papa?"

"That is what is called the sea anemone," he replied. "It is not a flower though, but an animal. It is said to have been called by the name of that flower about a hundred years ago by a celebrated investigator in the department of natural history, named Ellis. He thought it a suitable name because their tentacles are in regular circles and tinged with bright, lively colors, nearly representing some of our elegantly fringed flowers, such as the carnation, marigold, and anemone. As so they do while in the water and undisturbed. But when a receding tide leaves them on the shore, they contract into a jelly-like mass with a puckered hole in the top. There," pointing it out, "is the most common of the British species of sea anemone. It attaches itself to rocks and stones from low water almost to high-water mark. The tentacula—these feelers that look like the fringe of a flower—you see are nearly as long as the body is high and nearly of the same color. See, there is an azure line around the base, and on the base are dark green lines converging toward the center. Around the edge of the mouth is a circle of azure tubercles, like turquoise beads of the greatest beauty. I wish I could show them to you, but the mouth must be expanded in order to make them visible. Ah, that is just the thing!" as someone standing near threw in a bit of meat, which had the desired effect, the mouth of the anemone opening wide to receive it.

"Oh, they are very beautiful!" exclaimed Rosie, watching the appearance of the bead-like tubercles of which the captain had just spoken.

"Don't they eat anything but meat, papa?" asked young Neddie.

"Yes, crabs, sea worms, and fish. The tentacula are furnished with minute spears with which they wound their prey and probably convey poison into the wounds."

"I suppose this is salt water they are all in?" Walter said inquiringly, and he was told that he was correct in his conjecture.

On leaving the building they spent some time in examining its outside, finding its columns and arches wrought with calamus, fishes, frogs, serpents, and tortoises, making them appropriate and beautiful.

Chapter Sixteenth

"Papa, I wish we might go back to the Fair directly after supper and spend the evening there," Lucilla said, as again they stood on the *Dolphin's* deck. "I want so much to see the lighting up of the Court of Honor and then go to the wooded island to see it with the lamps lighted. After that, I would like to go the Ferris Wheel again to have the view from it by moonlight."

"Anything more, my child?" returned the captain with his pleasant smile.

"I think that would do for one evening, sir," she replied. "Unless my father would like to take me somewhere else."

"I think we will then come back through the Court of Honor and go to our beds," he said. "That is, should we make the visits proposed, which will depend at least somewhat upon the wishes of others in the party. Violet, my dear, how does that program suit you?"

"I really do not know of any way of spending the evening that I should enjoy more," answered Violet. "Indeed, Lu and I were talking together of our desire to see those sights not longer ago than yesterday. And you, mother, would like it, would you not?" she asked, turning to Grandma Elsie.

"Very much!" was the reply. "The tired little ones will be left in their beds, of course?"

"Yes, indeed! They will be ready for that as soon as they have had their supper," Violet replied with a loving look into each weary little face. "Come, dears, we will go to our stateroom, wash hands and faces, and smooth your hair. By that time supper will be on the table."

Everyone of the company approved of Lucilla's plan for the spending of the evening, and before the sun had quite set they were again in the Court of Honor. They were in season to secure seats from which they could get a good view of the lighting up.

They found there were thousands of people who seemed as anxious as themselves to witness the sudden change from deepening twilight to the grand illumination that made a fairyland of the Court of Honor. They were there for some minutes, sitting silently in the growing darkness, finding the buildings taking on a new beauty by the dim, uncertain light, and feeling it pleasant just to rest. They listened to the subdued hum of the thousands of voices of the multitude thronging about the white railing guarding the fountains, the doorways, the stone steps leading down to the water, and every other place where a human creature could find room to sit down and rest while waiting for the sight of the lighting up.

There seemed no ill humor among the great throng—no loud, angry talk, but a subdued buzz like many telephone messages coming over the wire at the same time.

The party sat where they could see both the Administration Dome and the Golden Statue at the other end of the lagoon. They had remained seated in silence there for some minutes, the darkness deepening, when suddenly there was a blare of music, the fountains threw up a few thin columns of spray, the front of a dark building was instantly illumined with a thousand jewel-like lights, then another and another blazed out in the same manner till all were alight with tiny jets of flame. Three rows, the first or highest following the cornices all round the court—these were of a golden hue, while some distance lower down was a second silver-colored row. Then the last, ranged just under the parapet of the lagoon, were golden like the first. The mingled light of all three shone on the dark waters of the lagoon, the gondolas skimming silently to and fro and the electric launches gliding swiftly onward.

The great dome of the Administration Building looked grandly beautiful with its line of flaming torches about its base, its triumphal arches of glittering fire above, and the golden crown sparkling on its summit. Great searchlights were flaming out from the ends of the Main Building, making visible the lovely seated Liberty in the MacMonnie fountain, as it foamed and rustled. Then, suddenly the two electric fountains sent up tall columns of water that changed from white to yellow, from that to purple, then to crimson, and from that to a lovely emerald green.

"Oh, it is just too beautiful!" exclaimed Rosie. "Too lovely for anything. I feel as if I could never weary of gazing upon it."

"No, nor I," murmured Evelyn in low, moved tones. "I never imagined anything so very beautiful in the world!"

"No, nor did I, and yet it cannot be anything compared to heaven," said Grandma Elsie. "'For eye hath not seen nor ear heard, neither have entered into the heart of man the things which God hath prepared for them that love Him!'"

They sat for some time gazing upon the amazing, enchanting scene. The party then rose and, still keeping together, wandered on till they reached the wooded island.

The scene there was lovelier than in the daylight. Little glass cups of various colors held tiny lights of wick in oil, giving a charming appearance to the scene, and there were thousands of visitors moving here and there among them.

So did the party from the *Dolphin* for a half hour or more. Then they returned to Midway Plaisance, and finding that the moon had risen, they sought the Ferris Wheel. Ascending in it, they had a beautiful view of the White City, the lake beyond, and the surrounding country. They made the circuit several times, and then leaving the wheel, they wandered slowly through the fairylike scene that lay between them and the Peristyle where the young men who lodged on shore bade goodnight and the others entered their waiting boat and returned for the night to their floating home. All were weary with the day's sightseeing and soon retired to their staterooms. But Lucilla, noticing that her father had remained on deck, hastened back again for a bit of the private chat with him of which she was so fond but in these days could so seldom get. He welcomed her with a smile. Drawing her into his arms, he added a tender fatherly caress.

"And what has my little girl, my dear eldest daughter, to say to her father tonight?" he asked.

"Oh, not very much of anything, papa," she replied. "But I'm hungry for a chance to hug and kiss my dear father without anybody nearby to criticize," she concluded with a low, happy laugh.

"Very well, my darling, you have my permission to do all you care to in that line," he said, patting her cheek and pressing his lips to it again and again. "I haven't lost the first place in my little girl's heart yet?"

"No, indeed, papa. And you need not have the least bit of fear that you ever will."

"That is good news—if something I have heard so many times can be properly called news."

"Are you tired of hearing it, father dear?" she asked half entreatingly, half incredulously.

"Indeed no, my darling," he returned, holding her close. "I can hardly bear to think there will ever be a time when I shall have to relinquish the very first place in your heart. Though I do not believe the time will ever come when your love for me will fail entirely or even be very small."

"I can't believe there is the very least danger of that, my own dear, dear father," she returned earnestly. "Oh, it would break my heart to think that you would ever love me any less than you do now."

"It would take a great deal to lessen my love for you, dear one," he replied, repeating his caresses. "Has this been a happy and enjoyable day to you, my daughter?"

"Oh, very enjoyable, papa! What a delightful time we are having!"

"You will be almost sorry when the time comes for returning home?"

"Oh, no, sir! We have such a sweet home that I am always glad to get back to it when we have been away for a few weeks."

"But playtime will be over, and your studies must be renewed."

"And that, with such a cross, cross teacher whom nobody loves," she returned sportively, laying her head on his shoulder, for he had sat down, drawing her to his side and putting an arm about her waist.

"Indeed! I had thought it was your father who was to teach you."

"And you didn't know how cross and tyrannical he was?" she laughed.

"So cross and tyrannical that he says now that it is time his eldest daughter was in her bed."

"Oh, please don't say I must go just yet, papa!" she begged. "There are so many of us here that I can hardly ever get a word with you in private, and it is so very pleasant to get you all to myself, even it is for only a few minutes."

"Well," he said, taking out his watch, "you may have five–"

"Oh, papa," she interrupted eagerly, "say ten. Please do! And I'll try to be ever so good tomorrow," she concluded with a merry look and smile.

"Ten then, but not another one unless you want me to say you must stay here on the *Dolphin* and rest all day tomorrow."

"Oh, no, sir, please don't! That would be worse than being sent to bed immediately. I'll go without a word of objection, whenever you tell me to. But oh, papa, wasn't it lovely to see the Court of Honor lit up tonight? And what could have been more beautiful than the view from the Ferris Wheel?"

"They were fine sights, and I am glad you enjoyed them," he returned. "Tomorrow we will, I think, go into the Manufacturers' Building and make some purchases. Would you like to do that?"

"Oh, yes, sir! Yes, indeed! I want to get some gifts for Christine, Alma, and the others at home."

"I highly approve of that," he said. "I have no doubt we will be able to find something for each that will be acceptable. Now the ten minutes are up, daughter. So bid me goodnight and go to your room and get to bed as quickly as you can."

"Goodnight and pleasant dreams to you, my own dear, dear father," she returned, hugging him tightly for an instant, then hastened to do his bidding.

"I presume you will be ready to start out early, as usual?" the captain said at the breakfast table the next morning, adding with a quick glance about from one to another. "I am very happy to see that everyone is looking well and bright."

"As we are feeling," said Mr. Dinsmore. "And it is certainly cause for gratitude to the Giver of all good. What have you to propose in regard to our movements for the day, captain?"

"It makes but little difference to me where we go, so that all are content," replied Captain Raymond. "But if no one else cares to decide the question, I propose that our first visit be to the Manufacturers' Building. We have been there before, but there are thousands of things well worth our attention that we have not yet looked at."

"Oh, yes. Let us go there first," together responded several voices, and so it was decided.

They set out, as usual, shortly after leaving the table, found their young gentlemen friends waiting for them in the Peristyle, and all proceeded at once to the Manufacturers' Building.

It was easy to spend a long time there, and they did, visiting one section after another, admiring all that was worthy of admiration in the architecture and exhibits. They examined the German pavilion with its towers, domes, and arches, its Ionic pillars upholding golden eagles, the fountains at the base, the Germania group in hammered copper surmounting the highest pedestal, and, most beautiful and impressive of all, the great wrought iron gates that formed its main entrance and were considered the finest and most remarkable specimens of that kind of work ever seen in this country.

The pavilion of France next challenged their attention, being close at hand. In front of its arched entrance stood two blue and green vases, which they learned were from the national porcelain factories of Sevres and were both very handsome. That factory had sent about two thousand pieces of its beautiful and costly china. Most of them had been already sold, but the captain and his party secured a few.

Germany, France, and Great Britain occupied three great squares grouped around the central circle of the immense building. On the fourth square were the exhibits of the United States. Three New York firms had accepted the task of making their country's section such a pavilion as should maintain her dignity and reputation, and they had certainly succeeded in so doing. It was of the Doric order of architecture and was enriched with a pale color and a profusion of gold, while from the center of the façade rose a column to a height of one hundred feet, having a ball and eagle on the top.

"Oh, let us go in and look at the exhibits in here—those of our own country!" exclaimed Lucilla after some moments had been spent by their party in an admiring examination of the outside.

Such seemed to be the inclination of the others also, and they passed quickly in and about.

The exhibits of jewelry there seemed to be the one thing that seemed to have the greatest attraction for the young girls of the party, Lucilla especially. Her father presented her with a pin and ring that gave her great delight, nor was he less liberal to his wife or Gracie.

"Ah, ha! Um, hum! Ah, ha! I see, captain, that you believe in encouraging home industries," laughed Mr. Lilburn.

"Yes, sir, especially when they are the best," returned the captain good-humoredly. "I have been examining jewelry in the various foreign exhibits and find none to excel and few to even compare with those of these United States."

"Yes," said Harold. "Some of our countrymen excel in those things, as they do in the art of the silversmith. Look at those translucent enamels worked on silver fretwork—here in the Gorham exhibit—and those fine pitchers and vases made of silver worked into open engraved designs, having pieces of colored glass blown into it. And look here at these beautiful designs of Rockwood pottery and silver."

"And yonder is Tiffany's exhibit," said Evelyn. "He is one of our finest jewelers. Let us go and look at that exhibit."

There was no objection raised, but all followed her as she led the way to the pavilion of which she had spoken. They found it well worth examination, for none of them had ever seen a finer display or greater variety of precious stones in costly and beautiful settings.

Our friends lingered some time longer in what the young people called "our section." There were other fine collections from other cities, too numerous to mention and far too many to be seen and examined in one day, or even in several.

After a time, however, the little ones grew very weary and indeed all were ready to enjoy a rest. So an electric boat on the lagoon was entered, and they all spent quite a while upon the water.

After that, they had luncheon at a restaurant, and then went to see the Spanish caravels.

"What are caravels, papa?" asked little Elsie, as they went on their way.

"You'll see presently," he replied. "You have heard the story of the discovery of America. These little vessels we are going to see are made as nearly as possible like those Columbus came over in. The men who built them looked up old pictures and descriptions and made these vessels as exact a copy of the old ones as they could."

"Was it in Spain they made them, papa?"

"Yes. They sailed from Palos in Spain about a year ago, and exactly four hundred years from the time when Columbus sailed from there to look for the land he felt sure was here on this side of the ocean. They took, as nearly as they could, just the course he did. Finally, they came on to New York, where they had a part in the international review in April of 1893."

"That's this year, isn't it, papa?"

"Yes. The review took place last April, and after it they sailed for the St. Lawrence River, came round the lakes as we did, and here into this harbor."

"How many are there, papa?"

"Three, the Santa Maria—in which Columbus himself sailed—the Niña, and the Pinta. There they are, daughter," as at that moment they came in sight of the three small vessels.

"Why, how little they are!" she exclaimed. "They are not nearly so big as the *Illinois* that we see all the time from our deck."

"You are quite right about that," her father said with a smile.

"But what would anybody want with such little bits of ships?" she asked.

"Only to show people with what little vessels Columbus accomplished his great missionary work of discovering America."

"I'm very glad he discovered it," Elsie said with satisfaction. "Because if he hadn't, we couldn't have been here living in it."

"Unless somebody else had discovered it between that time and this, Elsie," laughed her Uncle Walter, overhearing her last remark.

All were interested in looking at the little vessels, but their curiosity was soon satisfied. They returned to the Court of Honor for a time and then went back to the *Dolphin*.

Chapter Seventeenth

It was late Sunday afternoon. Most of the *Dolphin's* passengers were in their own staterooms enjoying a Sabbath rest after the fatigue of the sightseeing of the past week, but Captain Raymond sat on the deck with Neddie on his knee and his three girls grouped about him. The father and daughters had each a Bible, for even little Elsie could read fluently now and had been given a Bible of her own, which she valued highly.

"Papa," she said, "you know you bade each of us to have a verse to recite to you today. May I say mine now?"

"Yes, and we will begin with the youngest today," he replied.

"But that's I, papa, your Neddie boy!" exclaimed the little fellow on his knee.

"Why, yes, to be sure! But I hardly expected him to have one," the captain returned with a fatherly smile down into the dear, little face upturned to his. "Let me hear it then, son!"

"It's only a very little one, papa. 'The Son of man hath power on earth to forgive sins.'"

"A very sweet verse. Does my little son know who said these words?"

"Grandma said they were Jesus' words. She taught me the verse."

"Yes, it was Jesus our Savior who said it, and do you know whom he meant by the Son of man?"

"Grandma said it was Himself, and that He can forgive all our sins and take away our love of sin and make us truly good—really holy."

"That is truely a blessed truth. To Him alone, to Jesus who was God and man both, we must go to get our sins forgiven and be taught to love holiness—that holiness without which no man can see the Lord."

"Now mine, papa," said Elsie. "'He that believeth on the Son hath everlasting life.' Doesn't that mean that to believe on Jesus will take us to heaven at last—when we die?"

"Yes. As soon as we really and truly believe on Him—trust and love Him, giving ourselves to Him and taking Him for our Saviour—He gives us a life that will last forever, so that we will always be His in this world and in the next. Dying will be but going home to our Father's house on high to be forever there with the Lord and free from sin, suffering, and death."

"Never any more naughtiness, and never any more pain or sickness," said Elsie, thoughtfully. "Oh, how delightful that will be!"

"Yes, and to be with Jesus and like Him," said Gracie softly. "This is my verse. 'We love Him because He first loved us.'"

"Oh, what love it was!" exclaimed her father. "'Beloved, let us love one another: for love is of God. He that loveth not knoweth not God; for God is love.'"

"I have the next three verses, papa," said Lucilla. "'In this was manifested the love of God toward us, because that God sent His only begotten Son into the world, that we might live through Him. Herein is love, not that we loved God, but that He loved us, and sent His Son to be the propitiation for our sins. Beloved, if God loved us, we ought also to love one another.'"

"Yes," said her father. "If we would be followers of Christ, He must be our example. He who did not sin, neither was guile found in His mouth. Who, when He was reviled, reviled not again. When he suffered, he threatened not, but committed himself to Him that judgeth righteously. He, who bore our sins in His own body on the tree, bore it all that we, being dead to sin, should live unto righteousness, by whose stripes ye were healed."

"What does that mean?" asked little Ned.

"That the dear Lord Jesus suffered in our place, taking the punishment for us—the punishment we deserved—and letting us have the life bought with His righteousness and His blood."

"What is righteousness, papa?" asked the little fellow, as he gazed up into his father's face.

"Holiness. Goodness. Jesus was perfectly holy, and those who truly love Him will be ever trying to be like Him. We will go from strength to strength till every one of them in Zion appears before God. That is, till they get to heaven, and there they will be so like Jesus that they will never sin any more."

"And what does that other part, 'by whose stripes ye are healed,' mean, papa?" asked Elsie.

"That Jesus suffered for the sins of His people, for there was no sin of His own that He need suffer for. And that because he bore the punishment in their stead, they will not have to bear it and will be delivered from the love of sin. That is the healing—the being made well of the disease of the love of sinning and freed from the vile nature that we are born with. Our first parents disobeyed God there in the Garden of Eden."

"God teaches His people to hate sin and try hard—asking help of Him—to forsake it and be always good, doing just what is right. Doesn't He, papa? That's what grandma says."

"Yes, dear child, it is what God teaches us in His Word, the Holy Bible."

"And He will send His Holy Spirit to help us, if we ask Him to?"

"Yes."

"But how can we know it, papa? We can't see the Holy Spirit."

"No, daughter, but we may know it by the help He gives us, and others will recognize the fact by the fruit of the Spirit seen in our lives. Lucilla, can you tell me what the fruit of the Spirit is?"

"Yes, sir. The Bible says, 'the fruit of the Spirit is love, joy, peace, longsuffering, gentleness, goodness, faith, meekness, and temperance.'"

"Yes, and 'against such there is no law.' Jesus has kept the law perfectly in their stead, and His righteousness being imputed to them, they are treated as if they had never broken the law—never sinned—but had been always holy and obedient to all the commands of God, as He was."

Elsie was looking very thoughtful. "I think I understand it now, papa," she said. "Jesus has kept God's law in our stead, and he bore the punishment for our breaking it, giving His goodness to us, so that we are treated just as if we had been really good when we haven't been good at all. That is what it means where it says, 'by whose stripes ye were healed.'"

"Yes, dear child, that is just it. Oh, how can we help loving Him more and serving Him better. I ask earnestly for a new heart, for He in the hearer and answerer of prayer. The Bible tells us so."

"It is so sweet to know it," said Gracie, speaking low and softly. "For He is always near and able to help us, no matter what our trouble may be."

"Yes," said her father. "'Call upon me in the day of trouble; I will deliver thee and thou shalt glorify me.' 'Then shall ye call upon Me, and I will hearken unto you. And ye shall go and pray unto Me, and I will hearken unto you. And ye shall seek Me, and find me, when ye shall search for Me with all your heart.' God looks at the heart, my children, and He will not hear and answer us if we approach Him with lip service only, not really wanting what we are asking for."

"Yes, papa," said Elsie. "But I do really want the new heart I ask Him for. So He will give it to me, won't He?"

"Yes, daughter, for he has said so, and his promises never fail."

"I want to go to mamma now," said Neddie, getting down from his father's knee.

"Yes, run along," said the captain. "Our lesson has been long enough for today, I think. Daughters, you are also at liberty to go now. You, my little Gracie, are looking weary, and I think it would be well for both you and Elsie to take a nap now. Lucilla may, too, if she wishes," he added with a kindly glance at her.

"Thank you, papa, but I do not care to," she answered, as the others hastened away. "The breeze makes it very pleasant here on deck."

"Yes, and you can rest nicely in one of those steamer chairs." Then, taking a keener look into her face, he said, "But something seems to be troubling you, dear child. Tell your father what it is, that he may help and comfort you," he added in very tender tones, taking her hands and drawing her to a seat close at his side.

"Oh, papa, it is that I am—I am afraid I have been deceiving myself and am not really a Christian," she said with a sob, hiding her face on his shoulder. "There is so little, if any, of the fruit of the Spirit in me—no gentleness, goodness, or meekness—though I do love Jesus and long to be like Him."

"In that case, dear child, I am sure you are one of his," he answered low and tenderly. "Love is put first in the list, and I have seen, to my great joy, a steady growth in you of longsuffering, gentleness, and meekness. Jesus said, 'By their fruits ye shall know them,' and I think that, though far from perfect, my dear, eldest daughter does show by her life that she is earnestly striving to bring forth in it the fruit of the Spirit. 'The path of the just is as a shining light that shineth more and more unto the perfect day.' We are not made perfect in a moment, but we are to grow in grace, becoming more and more like the Master. When the work of grace is at long last completed—so that we are made perfect in holiness—we do then immediately pass into glory to be forever with the Lord."

"Yes, papa. But, oh, I do so want you to pray for me that I will grow in grace every day and hour of my life."

"I will. I do, daughter, and you must pray for your father, too, for he is by no means perfect yet."

"Papa, you do seem perfect to me," she said with a look of reverent love up into his face. "I never forget you in my prayers; I never forget to thank God for giving me such a dear, kind father. Papa, are you never troubled with fears that you might be mistaken in thinking yourself a Christian? Oh, no! I am sure not. For how could you be when you are such a good Christian that no one, who sees you every day and knows you as your daughter does, could have the least doubt about it."

"My daughter looks at me with the partial eyes of filial love," he replied, tenderly smoothing her hair. "But I, too, in view of my sins and shortcomings, am sometimes sorely troubled by doubts and fears. But then I find peace and happiness in just giving myself anew to Jesus and asking Him to take me for His very own and deliver me from all my sins and fears. Then, knowing that He is the hearer and answerer of prayers, I can go on my way rejoicing. Can you not do the same?"

"Oh, yes, papa, I will. I remember now that you told me once to do so—to come then to Him and He would receive me, and I need not trouble about the question whether I had really come before. And I did and found, oh, such rest and peace!"

"Yes, my daughter. 'The peace of God which passeth all understanding! May it ever keep your heart and mind through Christ Jesus.'"

Chapter Eighteenth

"Where are we going today, papa?" asked little Elsie the next morning at the breakfast table.

"I do not know yet, my child," he replied. "I have been thinking," he continued, addressing the company in general, "that it would probably be better for us to break up into quite small parties, each going its own way, now that the Fair has become so very crowded."

"Yes," Mr. Dinsmore said. "I will take my wife and daughter with me, if they do not object. You, I presume, will do likewise with your own wife and children, and the others—Rosie, Walter, and Evelyn—can make up a third party and dispose of their time and efforts at sightseeing as they please."

At that, Mr. Lilburn turned toward Miss Annis Keith and said with a humorous look and smile, "You and I seem to be left entirely out of the calculation, Miss Keith. Shall we compose a fourth party and see what we can find to amuse and interest us?"

"Thank you, sir," she replied. "But are you sure I might not prove a hindrance and burden?"

"Quite sure, and your companionship, if I can secure it, will be all sufficient for me."

"Then we will consider the arrangement made, for I should be sorry indeed to intrude my companionship upon those who do not desire it," she said with sportive look at the captain.

"Cousin Ronald," said the latter gravely, "I think you owe me a vote of thanks for leaving Cousin Annis to you. I am sure it should be accounted a very generous thing for me to do."

"Certainly, captain, when you have only Cousin Vi, those two half grown daughters and two sweet children for your share," laughed Annis.

"As many as he can keep together," remarked Walter. "Well, I'm going off by myself, as I happen to know that Rosie and Evelyn have been already engaged by other escorts."

"Walter, you deserve to be left at home," said Rosie severely.

"At home?" laughed Walter. "You would have to get me there first."

"You know what I mean. This yacht is home to us while we are living on it."

"And a very pleasant one it is—a delightful place to rest in when one is tired, as I realize every evening when I come back to it from the Fair."

"Then we won't try to punish you by condemning you to imprisonment on it," said the captain.

"Papa, I should like to go to the Manufacturers' and Liberal Arts Building again today, unless the rest of our party prefers some other place," requested Gracie.

"That would suit me as well as any," said Violet.

"Me, also," added Lucilla.

"Then it shall be our destination," said her father.

The group of young men—Harold and Herbert Travilla, Chester and Frank Dinsmore, and Will

Croly—joined the party from the *Dolphin*, as usual, in the Peristyle. Good mornings were exchanged, and then they broke up into smaller parties and scattered in different directions. Captain Raymond with his wife and children went first into the great Manufacturers' and Liberal Arts Building, where they spent some hours in looking at such beautiful and interesting exhibits as they had not examined in former visits. They also made a good many purchases of gifts for each other, for friends and relatives and the caretakers left at home.

Chester was disappointed and chagrined that he was not invited to accompany them, particularly as it was his and Frank's last day at the Fair. But he joined Walter and Herbert, while Harold took charge of their mother, and the other young folks went off in couples.

"Where shall we betake ourselves, Miss Annis?" asked Mr. Lilburn.

"I think I should like to look at some of the lovely paintings in the Fine Arts Building, if you care to do so," replied Annis.

"I should like nothing better," he returned. "So we will go there first."

They spent all the morning there, as there were so many pictures worthy of long study that it was difficult to tear themselves away from any one of them.

"'The return of the Mayflower,'" read Mr. Lilburn, as they paused before a picture of a young girl standing upon the seashore, looking out eagerly over the water toward a sail which she saw in the distance. There was such an impatient and tender longing in her face that one knew it seemed almost impossible for her to wait the coming of some dear one she believed to be on board—one whose love and care were to shelter her from cold and storm and savage foes who might at any moment come upon and assail her.

"Ah, the dear lass is evidently hoping, expecting, and waiting for the coming of her lover," he said. "The happy man! What a joyous meeting it will be when the good ship comes to anchor, and he steps ashore to meet her loving welcome."

"Yes, I can imagine it," Annis said. "They have doubtless been separated for months or years, and a glad reunion awaits them if he is really upon the vessel she waits for."

For a moment they gazed in silence, and then with a sigh, he said, "She's a bonny lass, and doubtless he is a brave, well-favored, young fellow—both on the sunny side of life. While I—ah, Miss Annis, if I were but twenty years younger—"

"What then, Mr. Lilburn?" she asked sportively. "You would be looking about for such a sweet, young creature and trying to win her heart?"

"Not if I might hope to win that of the dear lady by my side," he returned in low, lover-like tones. "She is young enough and fair enough for me. Miss Annis, do you think I—I could ever make myself a place in your heart? I am no longer young, but there's an auld saying that 'it is better to be an auld man's darling than a young man's slave.'"

"I have not intended to be either," she answered, blushing deeply and drawing a little away from him. "Single life has its charms, and I am by no means sure that—that I care to—to give it up."

"I hope to be able some day to convince you that you do," he returned entreatingly, as she turned hastily away and moved on toward another picture.

She had liked the old gentleman very much, indeed. He was so genuinely kind and polite, so intelligent and well informed. He had evidently enjoyed her society, too, but she had never dreamed of this—that he would want her as a wife. She would sooner have thought of looking up to him in a daughterly way, but as he had said he wanted a wifely affection from her, could she—could she give it? For a brief space, her brain seemed in a whirl. She saw nothing or heard nothing that was going on about her. She could think of nothing but this surprising, astonishing offer, and she could not decide whether she could ever accept it or not. She could not, at that moment, and she rather thought she never could. She kept her face turned away from him, as he stood patiently waiting by her side. Both had lost interest in the paintings. He was watching her and saw that she was much disturbed. But he could not decide whether that disturbance was likely to be favorable to his suit or not. Presently he drew out his watch. "It is past noon, Miss Keith," he said. "Suppose we take a gondola and cross the pond to the Japanese Tea House, where we can get a lunch."

"I am willing, if you wish it," returned Annis in low, steady tones, but without giving him so much as a glimpse of her face. He caught sight of it, however, as they entered the boat. Their eyes met, and he was well satisfied that she was not altogether indifferent to his suit.

"I would like you and your little brother and sister to retire promptly to your berths, Gracie, and try to get a good nap," the captain said when they had reached the deck of the *Dolphin*. "And Cousin Annis, I hope you'll not think me impertinent if I advise you to do the same."

"Not at all," she returned with a smile. "It is just what I was intending to do. I have a slight headache, but I hope to sleep it off."

"I hope you may, indeed," he said in a kindly, sympathetic tone. "I presume it is the result of fatigue and that a few hours of rest and sleep will make all right again."

She went at once to her stateroom, and changing her dress for a loose wrapper, she lay down with the determination to forget everything in sleep. But thought was too busy in her brain; she was too much excited over the surprising offer made her that morning. She knew instinctively that Mr. Lilburn had not given up hope of securing what he had asked for and that his suit would be renewed at the first opportunity. What should she—what could she say? It was not the first offer she had had, but—no, the suitor was never so good, so noble, so— He was everything one could ask or desire, so what difference that he was old enough to be her father? But would his sons welcome her into the family? And her own dear ones—sisters, brothers, nieces, and nephews—be willing to part with her? Perhaps not, but surely they could do very well without her and he—the dear old gentleman—ought surely to be considered. If she could make his last days happier and more comfortable, it could not be wrong for her to do so. The others could be happy without her. Ah, perhaps they would soon almost forget her. And to be close to Elsie Travilla, her dearest friend and cousin. How pleasant it would be to live near enough for almost daily interaction with her!

"I will ask for guidance," she finally said half aloud. Rising, she knelt beside her couch, earnestly beseeching her best Friend to make her way plain before her face and to lead and guide her all her journey through. Then, calmed and quieted by casting her burden on the Lord, she lay down again and presently fell into a deep, sweet sleep.

She was awakened by a gentle tap on the door and then Violet's voice asking, "Can I come in for one moment, Cousin Annis?"

At that, she rose and opened the door, saying, "Indeed you can, Vi. But what—who—?" as Violet handed her a bunch of Scotch heather, her eyes dancing with mirth and pleasure as she did so, for at the sight of the flowers, a crimson flush had suddenly suffused Annis's cheek.

"You see what," she said. "The who is Cousin Ronald. Oh, Cousin Annis, I would be so glad if only you won't reject him! He's a dear old man. Almost too old for you, I acknowledge, but don't say no on that account. Be 'an old man's darling;' there's a dear! For then we'll have you close beside us in that lovely home of Beechwood."

A silent caress was Annis's only reply, and Violet slipped away, leaving her once more alone. For a brief space, Annis stood gazing down at the flowers in her hand with a tender smile on her lips, the roses coming and going on her cheek. They seemed to be whispering to her of priceless love and tenderness, for Mr. Lilburn was a hale, hearty man. He looked much younger than his years. Who could know, he might outlive her, but years of genial companionship might well be hoped for in this world to be eventually followed by a blissful eternity in another and better land. They were both followers of the same Master, traveling the same road toward the city which hath foundations, whose builder and maker is God. Yes, she did indeed love the dear old man. She knew it now, and her heart sang for joy as she hastened to array herself in the most becoming dress she had at hand and pinned his flowers in the bosom of her gown.

He was alone in the salon as she entered it, and turning at the sound of her light step, he came forward to greet her with outstretched hand, his eyes shining with pleasure at the sight of his flowers and the sweet, blushing face above them.

"Ah, my darling, you do not despise my little gift," he said low and tenderly, taking quiet possession of her hand. "May I hope you will show equal favor to the giver?"

"If—if you think—if you are sure, quite sure, you will never repent and grow weary of your choice," she stammered, speaking scarcely above her breath.

"Perfectly sure! My only fear is that I may fail to make this dear lady as happy as she might be with a younger and more attractive companion."

"I have never seen such an one yet," she said with a half smile. "And I do not fear to risk it. I shall be only too glad to do so," with a low laugh, "if you have no fear of being disappointed in me."

"Not a ghost of a fear!" he responded.

As he spoke, the door of Mrs. Travilla's stateroom opened, and she stepped out upon them. Catching sight of them standing there hand in hand, she was about to retreat into her room again, but Mr. Lilburn spoke.

"Congratulate me, Cousin Elsie, upon having won the heart of the sweetest lady in the land."

"I do. I do," Elsie said, coming forward and bestowing a warm embrace upon Annis. "And I could not have asked anything better, seeing it will bring one whom I so dearly love into our immediate neighborhood." Even as she spoke, they were joined by other members of the party, the news of the state of affairs was instantly conjectured by them, and joyful congratulations were showered upon Cousin Ronald, and tender embraces and words of love heaped upon Annis.

Mr. and Mrs. Dinsmore were there, but the young couples who had left the older people that morning and gone off to explore other parts of the Fair had not returned. Presently a slight commotion on deck followed by the sound of their voices told of their arrival, and in another minute they were in the salon. Will Croly, leading Rosie to her mother said, "Will you give this dear girl to me, Mrs. Travilla? She doesn't deny that she loves me, and she is more dear to me than words can tell."

"Then I cannot refuse," returned the mother with emotion. "Knowing as I do that you are all a mother could ask in a suitor for her dear daughter's hand. But do not ask me to part from her yet. She is—you are both—young enough to wait at least a year or two longer."

"So I think," said Rosie's grandfather, coming up and laying a hand on her shoulder. "It would be hard to rob my dear, eldest daughter of the last of her daughters—to say nothing about grandparents and brothers."

"Well, sir, I thank both her mother and yourself for your willingness to let her engage herself to me, but I at least shall find it a little hard to wait," said Croly. "I am well able to support a wife now, and—don't you think we know each other well enough and that early marriages are more likely to prove happy than later ones?"

"No, I don't agree to any such sentiment. Older folks may as reasonably look for happiness—perhaps a trifle more reasonably—than young ones."

The words seemed to be spoken by someone coming down the cabin stairway, and everybody turned to look at the speaker. But no one was there.

"Oh, that was Cousin Ronald!" exclaimed Violet with a merry look at him. "And no wonder, since he has gone courting again in his latter days."

"What! Is that possible?" exclaimed Mr. Hugh Lilburn in evident astonishment. "And who? Ah, I see and am well content," catching sight of Annis's sweet, blushing face. "Father, I offer my hearty congratulations to you."

A merry, lively scene followed then, and mutual congratulations were exchanged, jests and spirited retorts were indulged in, and in the midst of it all there were other arrivals. Walter returned, bringing with him the two Dinsmore brothers and the Conly brothers and their wives. They were all told the news, and the captain noticed that Chester cast a longing glance at Lulu. He then turned with an entreating one to him. But the captain shook his head in silent refusal, and Chester seemed to give it up. With another furtive glance at Lucilla, which she did not see, her attention being fully occupied with the others, he, too, joined in the mirthful congratulations and good wishes.

Chapter Nineteenth

UPON LEAVING THE supper table, the whole company resorted to the deck, where most of them spent the evening, being very weary with the sightseeing of the day and finding restful seats there. The view was interesting and enjoyable. Chester and his brother left early to take an evening train for the South.

"I am sorry for you that you must leave without having seen everything at the Fair, Chester," Lucilla said in bidding him good-bye. "But none of us can stay the necessary forty-two years. I'll see all I can, though, and I'll give you a full account of it after I get home. That is, if you care to come over to Woodburn and hear it."

"You may be sure I will, and I thank you, too," he returned, giving the pretty white hand she had put into his an affectionate squeeze. "Good-bye. I'm glad you have your father to take good care of you."

"So am I," she said with a happy laugh. "I'm sure there's no better caretaker in the world."

Somewhat later, Lucilla, sitting a little apart from the others on the deck, watched furtively the courting behavior toward each other of the newly engaged couples.

"A penny for your thoughts, Lu," said Violet, coming up from seeing her little ones in bed and taking a seat by Lucilla's side.

"Really, they are not worth it, Mamma Vi," laughed the young girl. "I was watching Rosie, and wondering how she could ever think of leaving such a dear mother as hers to—to marry and live with even so good and agreeable a young man as Mr. Croly."

"And what do you think of my leaving that very mother—the very best and dearest of mothers she is, too—for a husband when I was a full year younger than Rosie is now?" returned Violet with a mischievous twinkle of amusement in her eyes.

"Oh, that was to live with papa—the dearest and best of men! I can see how one might well forsake father and mother and everybody else to live with him, Mamma Vi."

"I agree with you," said Violet. "I do love my mother dearly, and it would break my heart to lose her. Yet, I love my husband still more."

"I don't believe I shall ever be able to say that," said Lulu emphatically. "I feel perfectly sure that I shall never love anybody else half so well as I do my own dear father."

"I know it would trouble him sorely to think you did," said Violet. "So I certainly hope that you will not think of such a thing for at least five or six years to come."

"Five or six years! Indeed, Mamma Vi, you may be sure I will never leave him while he lives. I know I could not be happy away from him. I have always looked to him for loving care and protection, and I hope that if ever he should grow old and feeble, I may be able to give the same to him."

"I can scarcely bear to think that that time will ever come," said Violet, gazing at her husband with loving, admiring eyes. "But I hope it is far off, for he really seems to have grown younger of late—since coming here to the Fair."

"I think so, too, Mamma Vi," said Lucilla. "Indeed, it does seem as though everybody is younger—they all look so happy and interested—at least until they get worn out, as one does with all the walking and the thousands of things to look at, feeling all the time in that you will miss the very things you would care the most to see."

"Yes, that is the fatiguing part of it. But we had a nice time today, Lu. Aren't you pleased with your own purchases?"

"Yes, indeed, Mamma Vi! I am sure Christine, Alma, and the others cannot fail to be delighted with the gifts we have for them. And papa has been so very generous in supplying Gracie and me with money. I hope Max will be pleased with all we bought for him. Poor, dear fellow! It is just an awful shame he couldn't have been allowed to come here with us."

"Yes, I regret it very much," said Violet. "It has been one great drawback upon our pleasure. Lu, do look at Cousin Annis! She seems to have grown ten years younger with happiness. I am so glad for her, and that we are to have her for a near neighbor."

"I, too, but judging from Mr. Lilburn's looks, I should say he is more glad than anybody else. Oh, I wish they would get married at once! Wouldn't it be fun, Mamma Vi, to have a wedding here on the yacht?"

"Yes, indeed! Here comes your father," as the captain rose and came toward them. "Let's suggest it to him and see what he thinks of the idea," she added, making room for him at her side.

"Thank you, my dear," he said, taking the offered seat. "You two seem to have found some very interesting topic of conversation. May I ask what it is?"

"We are ready to let you into the secret without waiting to be questioned," returned Violet. "We have been planning to have a wedding on board, should you and all the parties more particularly interested give consent."

"And who may they be?" he asked lightly. "Not that couple, I hope," glancing in the direction of Croly and his ladylove. "Rosie is, in my opinion, rather young to assume the cares and duties of married life."

"As you said before, quite forgetting how you coaxed and persuaded a still younger girl to undertake them under your supervision," laughed Violet. "Ah, Captain Raymond, have you forgotten that consistency is a jewel?"

"Ah, my dear, have you forgotten that one's circumstances alter cases?" he returned in sportive tone. "But allow me to remind you that you have not yet answered my question."

"It is the older couple of lovers that Lu and I are benevolently inclined to assist into the bonds of matrimony, my dear husband."

"Ah! Well, I am pleased with the idea, and I have no doubt that it will be an easy matter to secure the gentleman's consent. In regard to that of the lady, I am somewhat more doubtful."

"I presume," said Violet, " she will veto it at first. That would be only natural, but we may succeed in coaxing her into it."

"I should think that if they are going to get married, the sooner the better," observed Lucilla gravely, as she looked on again at the lovers.

"Why so, daughter?" asked the captain.

"Because neither is very young, you know, papa. They can hardly expect to have many years to live together, and the longer they wait the shorter the time will be."

"Of their life together on earth, yes, but being Christians, they may hope to spend a most blessed eternity in each other's society."

"Shall we make any move in the matter tonight, my dear?" asked Violet.

"I think not, except to talk it over with your mother and grandparents."

"Yes, that will be a good plan," said Violet. "And mother will be the one to make the suggestion to Cousin Annis and persuade her to adopt it."

"Yes, for I am certain there will be no need of any persuasion for the gentleman's share in the matter."

"There, the Conlys are making a move as if about to go," said Lucilla. "And I hope they will, for I do want to know what Grandma Elsie and the others will think of the plan."

"Always in a hurry, daughter mine," the captain said, giving her an amused smile as they rose and went forward to speed the parting guests and assure them of a hearty welcome whenever they should see fit to return.

Not long after their departure, the others of their party retired to their staterooms, Violet, however, going first into that of her mother to tell of her own and her husband's plans concerning the nuptials of their cousins, Mr. Lilburn and Annis.

"That would be quite romantic for the youthful pair," Mrs. Travilla said with her low, sweet laugh. "I doubt very much, however, if you can persuade Annis to give her consent to so sudden a relinquishment of all the rights and privileges of maidenhood. Besides, she will hardly like to deprive her brothers, sisters, nieces, and nephews of the pleasure of witnessing the ceremony."

"They might be invited to come and be present at the marriage," Violet suggested a little doubtfully.

"I fear there are too many of them," her mother said in reply. "So that they will think it would be far easier for Annis to go to them and more suitable for her to be married in her own old home."

"Do you really think so, mamma? Well, please don't suggest it to her. I am sure that if our plan can be carried out it will be a great savings to them of both expense and trouble—for, of course, my husband would provide the wedding feast."

"Well, dear, I should like to see your plan carried out, and I must insist upon sharing the expense. But we will talk it over again in the morning. We are both weary now and ought to go at once to our beds."

"Then goodnight, mamma, dear. May you sleep sweetly and peacefully and wake again fully rested," Violet said, giving her mother a fond embrace.

"And you also, daughter. May He who neither slumbers nor sleeps have you and yours in His safe keeping through the silent watches of the night," responded her mother, returning the embrace.

The captain had lingered on the deck as usual to give his orders for the night, and Lucilla waited about for a bit of the private time with him of which she was so fond.

"Ah, so you are still here, daughter!" he said in his usual kind, fatherly tones as he turned and found her at his side. "Have you something to say to your father?" putting his arm about her and holding her close as something precious.

"Only the usual story—that I love my father very dearly and don't like to go to bed without telling him so and getting a fatherly caress."

He laughed, bestowing them without stint, and asked, "Is my little girl unhappy, about—anything, and wanting her father to comfort her?" he asked, looking keenly into her face.

"Unhappy, father? Here in your arms, perfectly certain of your dear love?" she exclaimed, lifting to his eyes full of joy and love. "No, indeed! I don't believe there is a happier girl in the land or in the whole world for that matter. Oh, you are so good to me and all your children! How very generous you were today to Gracie and me in letting us buy so many lovely presents to carry home with us. I am often afraid, papa, that you do without things to give the more to us. Oh, I hope you don't!"

"You need not be at all troubled on that score," he said, patting her cheek and smiling down into her eyes. "I have abundance of means and can well allow my daughters such pleasures. 'It is more blessed to give than to receive,' and when I give to you, and you use my gift in procuring something for another, it gives us both a taste of that sort of blessedness."

"So it does, papa. Oh, what a good place this is for making purchases! There are so many, many lovely things to be found in the various buildings."

"And we meet so many relatives and dear friends from various quarters. But that also gives us the pain of a good many partings," and again he looked keenly at her as he spoke.

"Yes, sir," she said. "But one can always hope to meet again with those one cares particularly about. So, I don't feel that I need to mourn while I have you, my dear father, and Mamma Vi and the little brother and sisters left. I am content and more than content, except that I do miss dear Max and can't help wishing he were here to see and enjoy all that we do."

"Yes, the dear boy! I wish he could be," sighed the captain. Then, with another caress, "Go now to your bed, daughter. It is high time you were there," he said.

"Just one minute more, please, papa, dear," She entreated with her arm about his neck. "Oh, I can't understand how Rosie can think of leaving her mother for Mr. Croly or any other man. I could never, never want to leave you for anybody else in the wide world."

"I am glad and thankful to hear it, dear child," he said with another tender caress and goodnight.

Chapter Twentieth

CIRCUMSTANCES SEEMED to favor the scheme of the captain, Violet, and Lucilla, for the family and their guests had scarcely left the breakfast table when there was a new arrival, a boat hailing the yacht and discharging several passengers, who proved to be Annis's sisters, Mildred and Zillah, and her brother, the Reverend Cyril Keith.

It was an unexpected arrival, but they were most cordially welcomed and urgently invited to spend as much of their time on the yacht as could be spared from sightseeing on shore. They were, of course, soon introduced to Mr. Lilburn—already known to them by reputation—and presently informed of the state of affairs between him and their sister. They were decidedly pleased with the old gentleman, yet they were grieved at the thought of so wide a separation between their dear, younger sister and themselves.

Violet, afterward seizing an opportunity when neither Mr. Lilburn nor Annis was near, told of her plans in regard to the wedding, adding that the subject had not yet been mentioned to Annis, but that she herself hoped no objection would be raised. It seemed to her that Cyril's arrival, thus providing a minister to perform the ceremony, the very one Annis would have chosen, of course, seemed quite providential to Violet's plans.

At first, both brother and sisters were decidedly opposed to it, for they wanted Annis to be married at home where all the family could be gathered to witness the ceremony. They felt it bad enough to lose her without being deprived of that privilege. Besides time and thought must be given to the preparation of a suitable trousseau. But, in the course of a day or two, they were won over to the plan.

But then the consent of those most particularly interested had to be gained. There was no difficulty so far as concerned Mr. Lilburn. He was really delighted with the idea, but Annis at first positively refused. She wished to be married at home, and she must have a trousseau—not that she cared so much about it herself, but Mr. Lilburn must not be disgraced by a bride not suitably adorned.

"Well, Annis, dear," said Mildred, who was the one selected for the task of obtaining her consent to the proposed plan, "you shall have all that you desire in the way of dress. I would not have you do without a single thing you want or think would be suitable and becoming. You shall have an abundance of money to make such purchases without applying to your husband for any one of them. You have some money of your own, I know, but it will be a great pleasure to your brothers and sisters to give to the dear girl, who was such a help and comfort to our loved father and mother, anything and everything she wants and will accept at our hands."

"Yes, I know I have both the best and kindest of brothers and sisters, and oh, I can hardly keep the tears back when I think of the separation that awaits us," said Annis with a sob, putting her arms around Mildred's neck and clinging to her.

"Yes, dear, I know. I feel just the same, though I believe you will be happy with the kind, genial gentleman who is stealing you away from us. But I can see that he is in great haste to get full possession of his little ladylove—at which I do not wonder at all—and I really think it would be better to take the plunge into matrimony suddenly and have it over," she added with a smile.

"Have what over?" asked Annis, smiling faintly.

"Not the matrimony," laughed her sister, "but the plunge into it."

"Oh, Milly dear, you wouldn't have liked to be hurried so!"

"Ah, but wasn't I?" laughed Mildred. "And I was rushed by this very brother of ours who expects to perform the ceremony for you!"

"Ah, I don't remember about that," returned Annis in a tone of inquiry.

"No, you were such a little girl then that I don't wonder that it has slipped your memory. But Cyril was about starting for college and so determined to see me married, so fearful that he would miss the sight if he went off beforehand, that he coaxed, planned, and insisted till he actually gained his point, hurrying me into wedlock before I had even one wedding dress made up."

"Oh, yes! And you were married in mother's wedding dress, I remember now. But, Milly, I haven't a single handsome dress with me! I did not think they would be at all suitable to wear in tramping about the White City and its buildings or needed in the hotel, where I spent but little time except at night. And so far, what I brought with me has answered every purpose."

"Never mind," said Mildred. "Handsome and ready-made dresses can be bought in Chicago, and it will not take long to procure one. You will, of course, want to select one that is well fitting and becoming in color. Gray would, I think, be very becoming and altogether suitable for a—not very young bride."

"No, I do not want to be too youthfully dressed or to look too bride-like on my wedding tour. So, I think I will have a dark navy blue."

"So, she has about consented to the desired arrangement," said Mildred, a little triumphantly to herself. Then aloud, she said, "Yes, that will be quite as becoming and a trifle more suitable, but let us go and talk it over with our cousins, Rose, Elsie, and Vi."

"There is no hurry," said Annis, blushing. "If I should give up to you enough to consent to have the ceremony performed here on the yacht, I shall put it off till the very last day of our stay, for I don't intend to miss seeing all that I possibly can of you, Cyril, Zillah, and the Fair."

"Very well," Mildred answered. "I incline to think myself that that would be the best plan, for really I want to see all I can of the dear sister who is going to leave us. Oh, Annis, dear, whatever shall I do without you!" she exclaimed, putting an arm about her and kissing her with tears in her eyes. "Ah, it seems that in this world we cannot have any unalloyed good!"

"No, Milly, dear sister, but when we get home to the Father's house on high, there will be no more partings, no sorrow, no sin—nothing at all but everlasting joy and peace and love.

"'Tis there we'll meet
At Jesus' feet,
When we meet to part no more.'

"Oh, doesn't it sometimes seem as if you could hardly wait for the time when you will be there with all the dear ones gone before—there at the Master's feet, seeing Him and bearing His image, being like Him, for we shall see Him as He is?"

"Yes, there are times when I do, and yet I am glad to stay a little longer in this world for the sake of husband and children and to work for the Master, too, doing what I can to bring others to Him. I want some jewels in the crown I cast at His dear feet."

"Yes, and so do I." A moment of silence followed.

Then Mildred said, "Let us go now and have our talk with the cousins, for it will not be very long before we will be summoned to the supper table."

Annis made no objection, and they went up to the deck, where they found the three ladies they sought—Zillah with them, too—sitting in a little group apart from the young girls and gentlemen.

They joined the group, and Mildred quickly and briefly reported Annis's decision. All approved, saying they would be very glad to keep her to the last minute and that there was a good deal more well worth looking at in the fair than she had already seen. Also, the delay would give plenty of time for the selection of a wedding dress and other needed articles of apparel.

"I shall go now and relieve the anxiety of the gentlemen, particularly the one belonging especially to me," said Violet in a lively tone, rising with the last word and hurrying away in their direction. The others sat silently watching her and her listeners.

"Ah," laughed Mildred presently, "they are all well satisfied with the arrangement except Mr. Lilburn. He wears quite a dubious, disappointed look. Ah, Annis, how can you have the heart to disappoint him so?"

"Never mind, Annis, he will prize you all the more for not being able to get possession of you too quickly and easily," said Mrs. Dinsmore.

"So I think," returned Annis demurely. "It will be quite as well for him to have a little more time to learn about all my faults and failings."

"I do not believe he will be able to find them," said Mrs. Dinsmore with an admiring look into the sweet face of the speaker, "since I have not succeeded in so doing."

Lucilla and Gracie, seated a little apart from the others, had been watching with keen interest all that passed among both ladies and gentlemen.

"There, just look at Cousin Ronald!" exclaimed Lucilla. "He isn't smiling and looks rather disappointed, I think. So, I suppose, we are not to be allowed to carry out our plan. But I think it would be just splendid to have a wedding here on board our yacht."

"Yes. So do I," returned Gracie. "But I suppose she doesn't like the idea of being married in a hurry. I'm sure I shouldn't. I don't believe Rosie would mind that, though, and Mr. Croly seems to say by his looks that he would like to take possession of her as soon as possible."

"Yes, no doubt he would. He ought to wait till he can have his father and mother present, however. Besides, Grandpa Dinsmore and Grandma Elsie won't consent to let her marry for at least a year. I shouldn't think she would be willing to leave her mother even then, unless as Mamma Vi did, for such a man as our father."

"But there isn't any other," asserted Gracie more positively than she often spoke. "Papa is just one by himself for lovableness, goodness, kindness—oh, everything that is admirable in a man!"

"Indeed he is all that!" responded Lucilla quite heartily. "Oh, I could never bear to leave him and cannot help wondering at Rosie—how she can even think of leaving her mother! Her father being dead, she wouldn't be leaving him, but Grandma Elsie is so sweet and lovable. But to be sure, just as I said, Mamma Vi did leave her. That seems all right, though, since it was for love of papa. But what are you looking so searchingly at me for, Gracie?"

"Oh, something that Rosie said last night quite astonished me, and I was wondering if it were at all possible she could be right."

"Right about what?"

"Why, that Chester Dinsmore is deeply in love with you, and that you, Lu, care something for him, as well."

"Oh, that is nonsense!" exclaimed Lucilla with a half vexed, yet mirthful look. "I am only half grown up, as papa always says, and really I don't care a lick for that young man. I like him quite well as a friend, as he has always been very polite and kind to me since that time he came so near cutting my fingers off with his skates, but it is absurd to think he wants to be anything more than a friend. Besides, papa doesn't want me to think about beaux for years to come, and I don't want to, either."

"I believe you, Lu," said Gracie. "You are as perfectly truthful a person as anybody could be. Besides, I know I love our father too dearly ever to want to leave him for the best man that ever lived. There couldn't be a better one than he is or one who could have a more unselfish love for you and me."

"Exactly what I think," returned Lucilla. "There's the call to supper."

Chapter Twenty-First

"ANNIS, DEAR, my ain love, my bonny lass," Mr. Lilburn said, when at last he could get a moment's private chat with her, "why condemn me to wait longer for my sweet, young wife? Is it that you fear to trust your happiness to my keeping?"

"Oh, no, not that," she replied, casting down her eyes and turning away her face to hide the vivid blush that mantled her cheek. "But you hardly know yet, hardly understand, what a risk you run in asking me to share your life."

"Ah," he said, "my only fear is that you may be disappointed in me. But if so, it shall not be for lack of love and tenderest care, for to me it seems that no dearer, sweeter lass ever trod this earth."

"Ah, you don't know me!" she repeated with a slight smile. "I am not afraid to trust you, and yet I think it would be better for us to wait a little and enjoy the days of courtship. One reason why I would defer matters is that we will never again have an opportunity to see this wonderful Fair, and I have seen but little of it yet. Also, I am not willing to miss spending as much time as possible with my dear brother and sisters whom I am about to leave for a home with you. I must make some preparation in the matter of dress, too."

"Ah, well, my bonny lass, 'if a woman will, she will you may depend on't, and if she won't, she won't and there's an end on't.' So I'll even give up to you, comforting mysel' that ye'll be mine at last. And that in the meantime I shall have your dear companionship while together we explore the streets and buildings of this wonderful White City."

At that moment others came upon the scene and put an end to the private talk.

The next two weeks were those of delightful experience to all these friends, to Annis in particular. She spent it in visits to that beautiful Court of Honor and to various interesting exhibits to be found in other parts of the Fair with an occasional change of scene and occupation by a shopping excursion to Chicago in search of wedding finery.

She would not allow herself to anticipate the pain of the partings from the dear brothers and sisters, nieces and nephews that lay before her, but she gave herself up to the enjoyment of the present with him who was the chosen companion of her future life on earth.

The yacht simply could not furnish nightly accommodations for all, but usually all the relatives and friends gathered about its supper table and afterward spent an hour or more upon its deck in rest that was particularly enjoyable after the day's exertion and in cheerful chat over their varied experiences since separating in the morning—now they were certainly much too large a company to keep together in their wanderings in and about the White City.

The time approached when they must separate, however. The trousseau—with the exception of such articles as it was considered more desirable to purchase in New York or Philadelphia—was ready, all the arrangements for the wedding feast had been made, and but a day or two intervened between that and the one which was to see Annis become a bride and set out upon her wedding tour.

The evening meal was over, and leaving the table they assembled upon the deck.

"Has anyone seen either the evening paper or the morning one?" asked Mr. Dinsmore, addressing his query to the company in general.

"Yes, sir, I have," answered Harold. "There was an awful railroad collision, one section of the train running into another. A good many were killed, one lady meeting with a most terrible fate," he added with emotion. "She was an earnest, active Christian worker, and no doubt she is now rejoicing before the throne of God."

"But oh, couldn't they have saved her?" asked his mother in tones tremulous with feeling. "How was it? What was the difficulty?"

"The car was crushed and broken, and her limbs caught between broken timbers in such a way that it was impossible to free her in season to prevent the flames—for the car was on fire—from burning her to death. The upper part of her body was free, and she close to a window, so that she could speak to the gathered crowd who, though greatly distressed by the sight of her agony, were powerless to help her. She sent messages to her dear ones and her Sunday school class and died like a martyr."

"Poor dear woman!" said Violet in low, tender tones. "Oh, how well that her peace was made with God before the accident, for she could do little thinking in such an agony of pain."

"Yes, and such sudden calls should make us all careful to be ready at any moment for the coming of the Master," said Mr. Dinsmore.

"Yes," assented the captain. "We do not know that He may not come at any moment for any of us, either in death or in the clouds of heaven. 'Be ye ready; for in such an hour as ye think not, the Son of Man cometh,' is His own warning to us all."

"Dear Christian woman, how happy she must be now!" said Grandma Elsie. "That agony of pain is all over, and an eternity of bliss at God's right hand—an eternity of the Master's love and presence—is already hers."

A moment of deep and solemn silence followed, then from the lake they seemed to hear two voices sweetly singing:

"I would not live always: I ask not to stay
Where storm after storm rises dark o'er the way;
The few lurid mornings that dawn on us here,
Are enough for life's woes, full enough for its cheer.

"I would not live always, thus fetter'd by sin,
Temptation without and corruption within:
E'en the rapture of pardon is mingled with fears,
And the cup of thanksgiving with penitent tears.

"I would not live always; no, welcome the tomb:
Since Jesus hath lain there, I dread not its gloom;
There, sweet by my rest, till he bid me arise
To hail Him in triumph descending the skies.

"Who, who would live always, away from his God;
Away from yon heaven, that blissful abode,
Where the rivers of pleasure flow o'er the bright plains,
And the noontide of glory eternally reigns;

"Where the saints of all ages in harmony meet,
Their Saviour and brethren, transported, to greet;
While the anthems of rapture unceasingly roll,
And the smile of the Lord is the feast of the soul."

Hugh Lilburn was present among the guests of the evening, and before the finishing of the first verse, the voices seemingly coming from the water had been recognized by more than one of the company as those of his father and himself. As the last notes died upon the air, a solemn silence again fell upon them all.

It was broken by Mrs. Travilla saying softly and in tones tremulous with emotion, "I have always loved that hymn of Muhlenberg's. Ah, who would wish to live always in this world of sin and sorrow, never entering, never seeing the many mansions Jesus has gone to prepare for those that love Him?"

As the last words left her lips, the two seemingly distant voices again rose in song, as the words came distinctly to every ear:

"Jerusalem the golden,
With milk and honey blest,
Beneath thy contemplation
Sink heart and voice opprest.
I know not, O I know not
What joys await us there,
What radiancy of glory,
What bliss beyond compare.

"They stand, those halls of Zion,
All jubilant with song,
And bright with many an angel,
And all the martyr throng.
The Prince is ever with them,
The daylight is serene;

The pastures of the blessed
Are decked in glorious sheen.

"There is the throne of David;
And there, from care released,
The shout of them that triumph,
The song of them that feast.
And they, who with their Leader,
Have conquered in the flight,
For ever and for ever
Are clad in robes of white.

"O sweet and blessed country,
The home of God's elect!
O sweet and blessed country,
That eager hearts expect!
Jesus, in mercy bring us
To that dear land of rest;
Who art, with God the Father,
And Spirit, ever blest."

"Thank you very much, gentlemen," said Mildred as the last notes died away. "What lovely words those are! Ah, they make one almost envious of that dear woman who has already reached that happy land where sin and sorrow are unknown."

"And death never enters," added Grandma Elsie low and feelingly. "Oh, 'blessed are the dead who die in the Lord.'"

Chapter Twenty-Second

THE WEDDING MORNING dawned both bright and clear. All the invited guests who had passed the night on shore were early arrivals upon the yacht, which then immediately started across the lake, heading for Michigan City.

The crew had outdone themselves in making everything about the vessel even more than ordinarily clean and bright, and everyone was arrayed in holiday attire. The young men of the party had taken care to provide an abundance of flowers, especially for the salon where the ceremony was to take place.

There they all assembled, drawn by the familiar strains of the *Bridal Chorus* from *Lohengrin* played by Violet on the small pipe organ, which the captain's thoughtfulness had provided for his wife's amusement and his own pleasure, as well as that of his daughters.

A hush fell upon them as Cyril entered and took his appointed place, followed closely by the bridal party, which consisted of Mr. and Mrs. Dinsmore and the bride and groom. Annis preferred to be without bridesmaids, and Mr. Dinsmore had expressed a desire to take a father's part and give her away.

The short and simple ceremony was soon over, and after the customary congratulations and good wishes, all repaired to the dining salon where they partook of a delicious breakfast.

All this time the vessel was speeding on her way, and the lake being calm and such breeze as there was, favorable, she made excellent headway, carrying them into their port in good season for catching their trains without being unpleasantly hurried.

The *Dolphin* then turned and retraced her course, arriving at her old station near the Peristyle before nightfall. The returning passengers were able to spend their evening, as usual, in the beautiful Court of Honor.

Captain Raymond and his wife and daughters returned to the yacht earlier than was their wont, and they sat together upon its deck awaiting the coming of the others.

"Papa," said Lucilla, breaking a momentary silence, "I have been wondering why we took the cousins to Michigan City rather than to Pleasant Plains as you did before."

"Because it would have taken a good deal longer to go to Pleasant Plains, for which reason they preferred Michigan City, not wishing to take the cars here because of the great crowds about the stations. Those crowds cause much inconvenience and even some peril to those who must push their way through them."

"I wondered myself that the bride and groom were at all willing to go on the cars after hearing of the many accidents on the trains as of late, papa," said Gracie.

"I trust they will not meet with any," said her father. "The crowds are coming in this direction, and I think it is on those trains that most of the accidents occur. But we will all pray for them, asking the Lord to have them in His kind care and keeping."

"Yes, indeed, papa!" she replied in earnest tones. "I am so glad that we may, and that we know—because He has told us so—that He is the hearer and answerer of prayer. Still I am glad we are not going home by rail."

"So am I," he said. "But yachts are sometimes wrecked, and in fact there is no place where we could be certain of safety except as our Heavenly Father cares for and protects us. In His kind care and keeping we are safe wherever we may be."